PALOMINO BLONDE
by Ted Allbeury

"Full of splendid know-how on an agent's inner and outer workings." —*The (London) Times*

Ted Allbeury

Palomino Blonde

PERENNIAL LIBRARY
Harper & Row, Publishers
New York, Cambridge, Philadelphia, San Francisco
London, Mexico City, São Paulo, Sydney

This book was first published by Peter Davies, Ltd., London, England. It is here reprinted by arrangement with Nat Soble Associates, Inc.

First PERENNIAL LIBRARY edition published 1983.

Library of Congress Cataloging in Publication Data

Allbeury, Ted.
  Palomino blonde.

  (Perennial library ; P/670)
  Reprint. Originally published: London : P. Davies, 1975.
  I. Title.
PR6051.L52P3 1983   823′.914   83-47576
ISBN 0-06-080670-2 (pbk.)

83 84 85 86 87 10 9 8 7 6 5 4 3 2 1

To my friends, Roger and Anne Coombs

PALOMINO BLONDE

CHAPTER I

The signpost said 'Bamburgh 15 miles' and the road turned
right just at the approach to Alnwick. At the old stone
bridge over the river he looked briefly to the north and
saw the massive rock-like structure of Alnwick Castle with
its dull brown pile frowning its disapproving domination
down the valley. Then, just as the careful instructions had
said, he accelerated up the hill, across the flyover where it
led over the A1 as it went north to Berwick. And then a
double S-bend, and a small lane turned off to the right at
the foot of a cottage garden. Almost hidden by cow-parsley
and ivy was a wooden sign with its white paint flaking so
that it was hard to read the faint black letters that had once
said clearly – 'RAF Boulmer'. The lane was narrow but
as the road curved to the crest of the rolling hills he could
see for miles on both sides of the low hedges. Looking east
he could see the white line of sand that was a deserted
beach, and then the dark blue of the sea. But over to the
south-east he could see the huge dish aerials, the big swing-
ing gondola sweep aerials and a forest of masts and pylons.
They looked near but they were almost two miles distant
and he guessed that by one means or another they would
already have him under observation.

There was no sign of life behind the barbed-wire fencing,
not even at the gate that was open near one of the guard-
houses. There were 250 men at RAF Boulmer, but for all
he could see the place was deserted. He ostentatiously
cleaned the screen of the green Mini and then started her
up and drove into Alnmouth.

Most of the boats were on their sides in the mud but
there were two or three still afloat in the main channel.
One was called *Patsy II*, one was handpainted with the
name *Ovadraft* and the third boat had no name at all. She
was in first-class condition and under a canvas cover in the
aft cockpit was a 150 h.p. outboard, double padlocked to a

bulkhead. The boat could do a hundred miles without a
refill and she was only going to do fifteen.

The green Mini coasted slowly to a stop. It was a dark
and cloudy night and without lights the man could only
use the grass verge as a guide. He had stopped the car
just beyond the big gate in the barbed wire, silently opened
the car door and after he had carefully stepped out he left
it open. He looked across at the guardhouse and the light
inside threw a pattern on to the grass that almost reached
the road. He watched the RAF sergeant inside speaking on
the telephone. It was the routine security call and after a
few moments the sergeant returned the phone to its cradle.
The watcher waited for another six minutes because it
was known that central security sometimes did a double
check at random just after routine calls. But nothing happened. As he moved forward the gun strapped against his
leg was catching clumsily and painfully against the side
of his knee. The silencer had put it out of balance. He
reached down as he walked and took the gun from its sling.
As he went through the gate he slid back the safety catch.
The guardhouse door was open and the sergeant was looking out. His hand was moving to the Smith & Wesson in
the canvas holster but two bullets had hit him before he
even touched it. The first one hit the base of his throat
and the second ploughed through his rib-cage and he was
dead before he hit the floor. The impact had thrown him
backwards and as he lay there spread-eagled, the man with
the Walther checked his pockets and found only a service
handkerchief. The black Nikkormat with the micro lens
was levelled at each wall of the guardhouse in turn, and
when the needle centred the shutter operated. When he had
finished there were only three shots left in the cassette.
Then he walked carefully back to the Mini, released the
hand-brake and pushed hard. As it gained momentum at
the downward curve of the hill he jumped in and held
the open door with one hand. He didn't swing it to until
he reached the crossroads to Alnmouth.

The man who rowed him out to the boat in the creek
helped him lift the small Meon anchor. The ebbing tide
pulled the boat eagerly and it was well clear of the creek

8

before he needed to start the outboard. The man who had rowed him out, beached the dinghy, and drove the Mini to Newcastle just before midnight.

There was a small but comfortable wooden shack available for the duty Special Branch Commander at RAF Boulmer and the present occupant was using the scrambler telephone to London.

'There hasn't been a full medical examination but it looks to me as if they used special nosed bullets, and they were probably cross-filed. The nose must have opened on impact because it churned its way through everything. It was a hell of a mess.'

'What makes you sure it's top pro?'

'The neck wound. That was first and it was to silence him. That was nickel tipped – I've already found it. That means the gun was loaded with two different types of bullet – one for his neck and one for his body. So it was somebody so sure of what they can do that they load a pistol accordingly. I'm guessing, but I'd say the shots were fired at 25 feet and that's pretty good shooting.'

'Anything removed?'

'No, nothing at all.'

'What action have you taken?'

'I've passed it to the County Constabulary at Morpeth and they're already here but I've told them to play it down.'

'Fair enough. Let me know any developments. What are you going to tell the press by the way?'

'Nothing, I've arranged a cover story here and the sergeant's body has gone to Edinburgh. Internally it's a confidential posting. I'm seeing the family later today and I can cover them all right.'

The United States National Security Agency monitoring unit in Grosvenor Square passed back a report to its HQ in Fort George Meade, Maryland, USA and later that day it was passed with 2,314 others to CIA Headquarters. It merely recorded that an unidentified small boat, estimated engine size under 300 h.p., had left the mouth of the River

Aln in Northumberland, and on a bearing of 073 degrees magnetic had made contact with the Soviet fishing boat *Pyotr Illyich* and had not returned.

CHAPTER II

There are some, men on whom the name Albert sits with
comfort and dignity. They are generally humble and frequently possess red hair and the bloodless freckled skin that
goes with it. Albert Edward Farrow was not one of these.
As soon as he was free of the pressures of family and
school registers he was Ed. Some, perhaps even experts,
would say that there is no difference in the images of
Alberts and Edwards. Theirs would be stamped the
ignorance of the pretentious, for if you mix with
Alberts and Edwards you would know they are as different
in character and promise as Mayfair and Soho. Or at least
as Shepherd's Bush and Soho.

Ed Farrow had left home when he was fourteen, mainly
to ensure the freedom to be out at night after 9.30 p.m.,
but if interrogated in depth would have had to agree that
freedom to live a wild life with the girls was at least a
vague incentive. In 1937, his wage of 45s. a week at age
eighteen was part of his reward for independence. An
ability to survive was another but he didn't yet know
that. By October 1939 Ed Farrow had recognized that
despite a lively mind and sound inbred instincts he was
not really cut out for the aggressive rat-race of business.
The army had much to offer, a better home than he had
outside, an identity and a peculiar kind of protection
against the world. Some knowing friends had smiled when
they heard of the move and talked of the army 'knocking
off the rough edges' and all that.

When Captain Ed Farrow left the army in 1946 he had
learned how to read a map, ride a motor-bike and drive
a car well, shoot 95's at 25 metres, jump with a parachute,
kill a man without sound or blood, and a number of other
things that made him a successful operator in SOE. Special
Operations Executive wanted Farrow to stay on after the
war when many of them were being absorbed into the
Special Intelligence Service. But Farrow had not been

tempted. He wanted to use some of his new skills and talents in a civilian role. MI6 had kept careful tabs on him for over five years and then something happened that caused them to send down an old hand to the boatyard near Maidenhead. Ed Farrow, like many others, had misjudged the post-war situation. Despite what the politicians had said, civilian employers preferred civilians to ex-soldiers, especially ex-soldiers who were tough as leather physically but vulnerable in a peculiar way mentally. The failing was hard to define, but put in a rough and ready way, those who had come back from the war seemed more gentle, less aggressive, than those who had stayed at home. And when every tuppenny ha'penny company was advertising for 'an aggressive this' or a 'dynamic that', talent and self-confidence were obviously not enough.

Ed Farrow knew a lot about radio and electronics and he had gone to the marine radio company after a couple of weeks of 'demob' leave. He had started as technical manager at a reasonable salary and for the next five years he had increased the salary and his responsibilities. The marine radio outfit was a subsidiary of a large group owned by a minor merchant bank. His income had increased through commissions on sales.

Life had been uneventful and strangely unfulfilling till he'd married Joanna, a quiet, attractive girl from Windsor. Then when young Joe had been born it was as if his batteries had been re-charged. Ed Farrow seemed to have found a new purpose, and life was suddenly sunny. They had a small cottage near the works at Maidenhead and Ed almost doubled his earnings in six months. His joy in the small boy and the gentle girl was visible and obvious, and he was that pleasant phenomenon, a man who had all that he wanted and needed. Ed Farrow's small world stopped on the afternoon of 5 August 1952.

It actually ended at 3.09 p.m. but the police hadn't identified the bodies and traced Ed until 5.15 p.m. He had been a widower for over two hours without knowing it. When he let himself into the cottage that night he was probably the only drunk man in the country who was carrying a girl's straw hat with flowers around the brim, a basket with three tins of baby food and a plastic bag

12

of Tufty Tails napkins. The next day, frozen faced, he locked up the cottage and he never went back. He slept that night in the cabin of one of the boats at the yard.

The MI6 man had spoken to him after the funeral.

'Captain Farrow?'

The tired eyes had looked at the man's face as if through fog, and it had taken an effort for the words to be forced out.

'Yes, I'm Farrow, who are you?'

'Would you have a drink with me?'

Farrow's jacket collar was turned up as if to protect him from the wind and rain but it was a calm sunny day and there was a heat haze on the river. The wind and the rain were inside. He put the back of his hand to his mouth and then he turned to look back at the graves and the handful of people who stood there looking at him and wondering what to do. He turned back to the stranger. 'Say it again,' and there were tears running down his cheeks. The man said 'Let's walk to the pub by the bridge.' And he took Farrow's arm gently and they walked together to the bridge.

It had been a straightforward proposition. They wanted him back. It meant tax-free money, and promotion to major. And all found. He'd be living free to any standard he chose that fitted his work. He'd be employed on special duties and most of his time would be spent in Europe and the States. The service had looked after the sale of the cottage and its contents and they had settled things with the radio company. Farrow had gone back to London that night with the man from MI6. He had taken a few personal papers in a brown carrier bag which he had placed on the floor of the Austin-Healey, between his feet, as they made the journey back to London. It was nearly 7 p.m. when the car swept on to Horse Guards' Parade and over to the far corner.

There were two men watching them from a War Office window, one was in uniform. They watched Farrow get out of the car and stand, carrier bag in hand, like a child waiting to be told what to do. They saw him look up at the sky and then he looked down and his head stayed down as his companion led him towards the steps.

The one in uniform said 'My God, Walker, I hope we haven't made a mistake. He looks like walking wounded for God's sake.'

'He is walking wounded, general. But we haven't made a mistake. It would take most men a year to recover from this. Farrow'll do it in three months, and he's got at least six months' training ahead of him. Don't worry, he's the right man.'

For seven years Farrow had run a network in West Berlin, then there'd been five years in the States liaising with the CIA and the NSA, and a special stint in the Foreign Office covering the Soviet Union and all the satellites. Farrow was now in his seventh year in charge of all clandestine operations in East Berlin. Two years ago, for the first time, he had not realized that it was 5 August until eight in the evening.

Behind the door marked 'Department of Experimental Psychology' there was nothing but a bare room. It had an overpowering smell of fresh paint. The department was part of the psychology faculty of Leningrad State University. The faculty was housed in the same block as the history faculty and the economics faculty. Several other 'splinter' departments shared a handful of rooms in the far corner of the third floor. Outside was a low eighteenth-century arcade with small white pillars. The students who collected to read the notice boards and class schedules would pretend not to notice the pale blue uniforms of the unsmiling Soviet staff officers who walked slowly through the arcade towards the psychology faculty on the third floor.

On this particular day there were three officers and a civilian. They unlocked the door marked 'Department of Experimental Psychology' and one of them walked over to the window and opened the two long frames. He sat on the window-box and looked down to the university grounds for a moment, and then turned and spoke to the civilian.

'Well, Sergei Illyich Venturi, here is your room, and you heard at the meeting that you can call on any resources you require.'

The man he addressed looked about forty years old. Tall and slim and wearing a well-cut suit. His face was on the thin side, quite handsome in an actorish sort of way, but the eyes didn't fit. They were grey like slates and they didn't blink as they looked in turn at the other men.

'What does Boulmer mean?'

'Nothing at all so far as we know. It's just a place on the north-east coast.'

'And why do we think it will be there?'

'Well we're not sure. But that's where Hallet was moved to and he's the man. You'll see our evaluation in the files, and details of Hallet.'

'Right I'll say good-bye to you all now, and get started.' He bowed briefly in their direction, and then awkwardly and with some embarrassment they registered their dismissal and moved to the door.

Shortly afterwards he was giving instructions to a party of soldiers about the placing of tables and apparatus and several modern filing cabinets.

Sergei Venturi was actually thirty-nine, and an experienced operator in the KGB. He specialized in electronics but he had had a full range of KGB and navy training. He had been born just outside Leningrad where his father had worked all his life as a mechanic. As a child he had belonged to the Pioneers, graduated to the Komsomol, and became a Communist Party member at the age of twenty-one. After finishing elementary school Venturi had volunteered for the naval school on Vasilevsky Island. From the secondary naval school he was sent to the Frunze higher naval school, the Soviet Union's best. He had been one of the Red Navy's most brilliant young officers and had been given command of a Baltic Fleet destroyer at the age of twenty-six. A year later he had been given orders to report as naval attaché at the Tokyo embassy. He had been picked up in Moscow and had spent that evening and night at the Lubyanka complex, the headquarters of the NKVD. He had operated for the KGB in the United States, in Dublin and London.

On the night of 9 July 1953 he had been at the main

secretariat on Kuznetsky Most. Ten minutes after Kirill Moskalenko had gunned down Lavrenti Beria the hated boss of the NKVD, his phone had rung and he'd been ordered over to the Kremlin buildings. Moskalenko was still in the room, still holding a sub-machine gun. Kruschev was holding a bloody handkerchief to his hand and had said to Venturi, 'Comrade I'm told you were Red Navy and now you are NKVD.' Beria was lying on his back with an automatic in his left hand and his face and body were covered with blood. Kruschev kicked the dead man's foot and said 'Get this scum out of here comrade and put him where he won't be found – ever', and he'd turned to the others – Zhukov, Malinovsky, Molotov and Mikoyan – 'you agree?' There had been no dissenters.

Moskalenko had walked with him to the door. 'Burn the bastard – burn him tonight.' And that is what he had done. Six months later Moskalenko was made a Marshal of the Soviet Union, and in 1960 he was made Deputy Defence Minister in charge of Soviet rocket forces. Venturi had been promoted too, but more important he'd become an 'untouchable' and when the NKVD had become the KGB, Venturi had been transferred to the Red Army's intelligence service – the GRU. It was the GRU that worked Klaus Fuchs, the Rosenbergs, Lonsdale and Sorge, and Venturi was the youngest colonel the GRU had ever had.

CHAPTER III

George Sharp worked in the service department of the North Eastern Electricity Board and he spent most days stripping down cookers from council estates. It required some skill but it was monotonous, uninspiring work. Despite radio and TV discussions by experts on 'job enrichment' nobody had ever found a way of relieving the monotony of this kind of job. Not that George Sharp would have welcomed experiments. For George was a man who lived two lives. Most nights, George sat in the attic of his sister's house at Morpeth just north of Newcastle. And there George was the boss of G4XNE and he chatted on short-wave with fellow hams all over the world.

On the night of 24 July George had spent the early evening tuning his aerial and bringing his log up-to-date. He'd joined a network on the two-metre band which had kicked around the advantages of valves instead of transistors until midnight. He'd spent an hour working out the details of a mobile competition that his local radio club proposed organizing for sometime in the next month. Then at 01.15 GMT he was ready for the real stuff. George put on the headphones and turned up the RF knob on his receiver. It was a big Eddystone 940 and since he'd invested in his new aerial tuner it had been pulling in calls from all round the world. There was a CQ call from a man in Seattle and George switched the receiver to 'standby' and tuned in the transmitter. He glanced up at the big electric clock on the wall. It was 01.21 GMT precisely. As he turned the receiver tuner a few cycles the needle came up and he pressed the microphone 'speak' button. George Sharp saw only the first vivid, white, pulsing flash.

The US Army Air Force pilot had been given explicit instructions that the demonstration flying would not include handing over the controls to the RAF Wing Commander under any circumstances. It was a demonstration flight not an instruction flight and as the man from General Dynamics had said, 'Major – this little bundle is meant to impress these boys but it ain't for sale – so there'll be no touching and no explaining. It's just a ride.'

The plane was a modified General Dynamics FE-111E. At 40,000 feet it clocked up an easy 1,650 m.p.h. – two-and-a-half times the speed of sound. And that was with full combat load.

They had fired the full load of 3,000 rounds from the 20-mm. cannons over the North Sea, and then screamed over the English coast at King's Lynn and swept in a wide circle across the East Midlands and tore through the sky up to Yorkshire and County Durham. RAF Strike Command Air Control had heard a shout over the static and then there was silence.

The FE-111E crashed on the wild, heather-covered Cheviots just south of Rothbury. The subsequent service examination indicated that there had been spontaneous fire over all the aircraft with no apparent start point. The remains were shipped to Texas for the US Army Air Force to carry out its own investigations.

Two national newspapers reported an IRA bomb attack on a generating sub-station on the night of 24 July and that the Northumberland Constabulary were following several lines of inquiry.

In the room at the University of Leningrad Venturi was studying a 20 × 16 colour enlargement. It was slightly damp but it was crisp and sharp. It showed the back wall of the guard room at RAF Boulmer. Only the top half was covered, the rest was plain hardboard. The top half contained two quarto pages with typed instructions for the duty guard, facsimile examples of various identity cards, a list of top-secret telephone numbers and the triple page spread of Playmate of the Month for January 1973. The identity cards included those for Special Branch, MI5, MI6, the FBI and CIA, and the United States National Security Agency.

CHAPTER IV

Sergei Venturi was looking at the gate-fold in *Playboy* for January 1973. He had a specialist printer's report comparing the actual *Playboy* picture with its reproduction in the colour enlargement. The report said that the colour print had too much cyan and that would make the forgeries of the identity cards inaccurate. Not so inaccurate that anyone would notice, but Venturi was a meticulous man and he phoned through for the colour plates to be remade.

There were several piles of newspapers on one of the trestle tables. They were seven weeks' issues of the *Northumberland Gazette* with slip editions for Morpeth and Berwick and each day's issues of Newcastle's morning and evening papers, *The Journal* and *The Evening Chronicle*. On the wall were a number of identical copies of the same ordnance survey sheets covering Alnwick and the coast, and against one of them was a set of pasted-on newspaper cuttings with black cotton threads to various points on the map. The cuttings included the details of the crashed FE-111E; a death by misadventure verdict on an amateur radio operator, and some details of the fire which had destroyed half the house in which he had lived. There was a whole sheaf of reports linked to the RAF installation at Boulmer, including the names of two cricket teams, pictures of the commanding officer giving out presents at an old people's party and pictures and names of the parents of entrants in an RAF bonny babies contest.

There were several files on Venturi's curved white desk. One of these was marked Dr James Hallet PhD. It contained photographs of a man who looked about thirty-five years old. One was a newspaper photograph of Hallet outside Buckingham Palace with his wife and daughters. He was showing an OBE in its purple velvet-lined case. The others covered Hallet as a member of a tennis team at a Cambridge college, eating an ice-cream whilst leaning against the bridge in St. James's Park and several which showed him in various poses with a pretty brunette. Both were naked on a double bed and a small poodle lay with its head on the pillow as if bored with the goings on. There were over thirty pages of typescript giving details of Hallet's background and career.

Hallet was a product of middle-class parents and he had spent his youth in Wimbledon. All his life Hallet had had charm, and even his worst enemies, and there were regiments of those, would not attribute his academic and research successes to anything other than a brilliant scientific mind. The bitterness was always caused by his sarcastic dismissal of other work in his field, and was exacerbated by the fact that he was generally right. His researches on the atomic structure of conductivity had been done when he was in his early thirties. When the copper shortage came in the late 70s, it was Hallet with Anton Mayer who had patented and produced a plastic with superior conductivity to any known metal.

They had become multi-millionaires overnight and Hallet had not disguised his liking for pretty girls and fast cars. It was typical of the man that one of his first acts was to give a million dollars to the Frankenheim Foundation. The public saw it as a generous gift to a worthy cause, but every scientist saw it for what it was meant to be – a 'V' sign to all the charities and trusts that doled out money to top Western scientists to keep them at their benches.

He'd said on a TV interview that in the Soviet Union scientists didn't have to depend on charity or the bureaucratic whims of laymen to obtain funds to carry out their research. And it was assumed by the establishment that it was inside information that had provided his interesting data, that in the mid-70s thirty-two good scientists had left the West for the Soviet Union but only one had defected from behind the Iron Curtain.

On the other hand there had been continual rumours indicating an aggressive sexuality. Stories of girl students and mini indecencies hushed up by faculty heads or vice-chancellors. In Venturi's file there were most of the details, and a psychologist's report. There was a long bibliography

20

and an index of film clips, microtapes, tape-recordings and photostats of documents.

Lieutenant Joe Machin, United States Navy, looked at his watch and then looked over the stem of the boat to watch the movement of the nylon drogue anchor which was holding the 30-footer steady against the gentle roll of the waves. It was a clear hot day and over the stem he could just make out the faint outlines of home. Home was an atoll. In US Navy designation it was Atoll 197 and the young lieutenant did two months' duty on the atoll and then had a full month's leave. During the two months he lived comfortably but alone. Plenty of food, plenty of books, and a powerful transceiver that linked him straight into NSA HQ. Every twentieth day Machin would take out the boat to the fixed bearing that they gave him and he'd wait. Sometimes twenty minutes but never longer than an hour. Then the small black and yellow parachute would drift down and he'd lift it from the sea, put it in the special plastic bag and take it back to the hut. It would stay in the Frigidaire until the aircraft came next day.

The photographs in the containers were the product of the biggest jump forward in espionage in a hundred years. Some said that it marked the end of the secret agent, others reserved their judgement. Whichever school of thought was right Samos has a north-south orbit 300 miles above the earth, far beyond the reach of any existing weapon. It takes an Atlas rocket to get it up there but when it's there it circles the earth once every 95 minutes and its Kodak and Ansco cameras produce photographs with the same detail that a man can see from one side of the highway to another. They photograph the entire land mass of the Soviet Union and its satellites every five hours. They reveal every military move from troop concentrations to road traffic. In a nation of 214,000,000 people, only four people saw every Samos photograph, and three of them had never met. As for the United States' NATO allies, the photographs covered them at much greater intervals and only two men checked the interpretations. One of these was a CIA officer named George Lane.

21

George Lane was a bachelor from Wichita Falls, Texas. Nearly fifty he looked more like middle thirties. Slim, carelessly dressed and with a simple natural charm that made him impossible to dislike, he'd fought as a bomber pilot in the Korean war and it had taken a chunk out of his life at the wrong time and he'd come back with a love of airplanes and service life and the kind of respect for marriage that would preclude any normal mortal from trying it.

George Lane worked at the new, big CIA complex just outside Washington, in Langley, Virginia, and he was working late. He was making the interpretation of the Samos photographs covering Great Britain, Ireland, Scandinavia and the northern coast of Germany, and he'd got at least another hour's work to complete before he signed off. He looked at his watch. It was just 10 p.m., he automatically checked the time against the networked digital clock on the wall. It matched, and he stretched his arms and walked over to the coffee machine. Back at his desk he'd taken a couple of sips and bent once more over the big flat table.

He ran the magnifying carriage very slowly along the horizontal grid with his right hand and switched on the recorder that took down his comments. He was slowly dictating – '... apparent wave height 8 feet – new grid line – bearing zero one degrees, zero five minutes, five three point five seconds west – Northing five-six degrees, five six minutes and – hold it, hold it – a small vessel on bearing from Tynemouth repeat Tynemouth at zero seven eight degrees – configuration indicates British Navy tug – no visible crew – estimated rate of travel less than fifteen knots – estimated wind – Beaufort four, south-easterly – abnormal structure on aft flight deck. Doubling magnification from times seven to times fourteen – unsatisfactory due to grain break-up – reducing magnification to times two – yes this is O.K. – structure is winch – non-standard pattern – appears to be winding gear for hawser but roller empty – check – in fact hawser is paid out and I am moving to next grid south, next grid east – yes tug is making long tow to some structure – structure appears to have brilliant illumination – position is ...' and so it went on, covering the photographs for the night of 24/25 July.

*   *   *

James Hallet walked slowly out of the Guggenheim Gallery and shaded his eyes from the bright contrasty sun as he looked over to Central Park. Then his eye caught a cruising cab and despite some rival handbag waving by a couple of blue-rinse ladies, he was the lucky winner. As he settled back and said 'Grand Central' he pushed the exhibition catalogue into his brief-case. It was an exhibition of photographs – a crib of Edward Steichen's 'Family of Man' but with an over-coy emphasis on women and women photographers. It didn't come off and it left an impression that Margaret Cameron and Cecil Beaton were better than the new girls and boys. It amazed him that anyone had the nerve to rake up once again Robert Capa's Spanish soldier with arms outflung in the act of dying – was it naïveté or just indifference?

As he looked out of the cab, Park Avenue was at its Sunday best and he felt a positive, tangible joy as he thought over what he intended to do. First to Grand Central because the bookshop would be open and he wanted to stock up on light reading. Then back to the apartment on Fifth Avenue. A long, warm bath with a bottle of Dom Perignon on the cork topped table. And on the hi-fi some mood music for a sunny Sunday lunchtime, probably the Respighi tape with the Pines, the Birds, and the Fountains of Rome, and his mind translated it automatically as if it was an examination question. 'Gli Pini, gli Ucelli, e'le Fontane di Roma', and as the startled driver looked round he realized he'd said it aloud.

A few minutes later they were at the station and he sauntered through the concourse to the bookshop. The car that stopped behind his cab waited a few moments, then its passenger stepped out, and without comment walked into the station entrance. The car driver and the cab driver spoke for a few moments together and then drove off.

Hallet was bending down with his head on one side trying to read the titles on the spines of the lowest shelf of books when his eyes lighted first on a pair of white court shoes with accompanying ankles. Then his eyes moved up a superb pair of legs until his neck wouldn't bend any further. Then he stood up to get a better look. The girl was about twenty-two or so, with a cool, lovely face.

Brown eyes, full mouth and even teeth. She was tall and slim but as she reached upwards for a book Hallet's eyes went instinctively to the full breasts that lifted with her arm. Her blonde hair was almost silver and as he took in the brown eyes, the long black lashes and eyebrows he wondered if she were really blonde. The book fell and he scooped it up and offered it to her. It was Palgrave's *Golden Treasury* in a calf binding. 'I don't know whether you were putting it back or taking it down but here it is.' The big brown eyes looked at him and she was smiling and a word came into his mind – radiant. She was radiant – beautiful – stunning – and he heard a voice like a dove with a Scandinavian accent say, 'It must be a real, how you say it – Freudian slip. I want book but it's too much money so I go to put it back and it falls and here am I holding it again. I think I have to buy it now,' and the lovely head turned on the slim neck to look for an assistant. Very quickly he said 'May I buy it for you, it's an English book and I'm English. I'd like to do that.' She turned her face to look at him and after what seemed an hour's examination she said softly, 'Thank you, that would be very nice – and you write me something in English inside, yes?'

And so the deed was done and they'd had lunch at 'L'aiglon' and afterwards they'd gone to Central Park and walked across to the zoo and sat eating ice-creams, watching the apes eating bananas. It seemed she was in fact twenty-two, and she'd been in New York only ten days. She was staying with her aunt and uncle in an apartment on Lexington near the Waldorf Astoria and she was returning to Europe in about eight or nine days' time. And she wasn't Swedish she was Danish. He got the impression that the family were well off but she didn't talk about them very much. He gathered that her father had a factory making high-class hi-fi equipment. It was almost six when he saw her into a cab. They were going to meet in the Carousel at the Waldorf Astoria two hours later.

Back in his apartment he ran a bath and lay soaking for half an hour. The music he chose wasn't Respighi but Henry Mancini.

At the most she was five minutes late and when she

walked in the bar a silence fell. She wore a knitted dress in dazzling white wool which clung to her, and a necklace of superb pearls and they followed the line of her slender neck and came to rest in the deep cleavage that exposed most of her magnificent breasts. Her face, shoulders and arms looked like an expensive colour shot for an advertisement for Ambre Solaire. She walked like a racehorse walks, easily, fluidly and with a quiver of firm flesh. She wore a white fox stole with a platinum and diamond clasp and in one hand she held an embroidered evening bag and the Palgrave. As he walked towards her he wondered what it would take to get her into bed. Her hand went out to him and she was smiling, 'I bring my book – you forgot to write to me in it.'

She said she didn't drink but she sipped her way through a mild John Collins and at dinner they shared a bottle of Paul Masson's Pinot Noir and she wouldn't believe it was from California until he showed her the label.

When they were back at his apartment they were sitting together on the curved double settee. The lights were gentle but not low, and the music was there with lush strings. The girl put her head on one side listening, with one slim finger to her mouth, and then she smiled and nodded. 'Yes, it's the music from "Spartacus and Phrygia" by —' and she frowned and snapped her fingers, 'yes I got it – by Aram Khachachurian.' He looked up quickly from pouring a drink. 'My, that's pretty good – you must be a Russian music fan.' She smiled and she was blushing at his praise. She shrugged. 'No, I see the ballet in Stockholm last year. I like.' And then she'd picked up the Palgrave and leaning over she'd said 'Now you write something special just for me – just for us, yes?' He turned to the fly leaf and after a moment's thought he wrote:

'Oh if thy pride did not our joys controul,
What world of loving wonders should'st thou see!
For if I saw thee once transform'd in me,
Then in thy bosom I would pour my soul.'
To Kristina with love – New York – August.
James M. Hallet, PhD, OBE, London, England.

The girl read it slowly and then pointing to the abbreviations she asked what they meant and he told her. She looked at him and pushed out her lips. 'So you very clever – very important man and I waste your time.' He leaned across and kissed the bright red mouth and she slowly responded as his arms went round her, then after a few long moments she gently pushed him away. 'Is this Shakespeare this poetry?' His arm was still around her shoulders. 'No, it was written a long, long time ago by the Earl of Stirling, about 1595 – it's called "To Aurora" but I don't know who she was.' She pointed to the last line. 'What means soul?' He shrugged. 'It means spirit like *âme* in French or *Seele* in German.' She looked at the words again and then looked up at his face. 'And what means bosom?' The big melting brown eyes were close to his and the music had come to an end and he could hear his heart pumping in the silence. His hand moved forward and closed over one of the firm breasts as he said softly 'That's what it means.' Even when his fingers fondled the firm flesh she made no move to stop him. As his mouth moved on hers she sighed and relaxed, and a few moments later his hand was inside the white wool covering and his fingers enjoyed the smooth resilient flesh. The big brown eyes were open as his hands enjoyed her body. She watched his face and did nothing to stop him. Nearly ten minutes later he pulled her against him and after a few moments she said 'You want me like this very much Jimmy?' He nodded and his hand pulled her to him as he moved against her. She moved her body against his for a few moments and then she said 'We do this better in bed I think.' She had left after midnight and they had arranged to meet the next evening.

It had taken him five days to persuade her to come back with him to London. She'd raised the question of his wife and daughter but they had been dismissed out of hand. His vanity was fed because this beautiful creature was so obviously impressed by him, and his lust was fed by the pretty face and the full breasts and the long shapely legs that opened so eagerly to give him both excitement and relief. She persuaded him to stay in New York for another weekend and they flew back together on the late flight on

26

the Sunday evening. She said she had been to England twice before. Once on a school trip and once for a week's holiday in London when she was eighteen.

He carried their bags to the car-park and she was obviously impressed with the white Lamborghini. There was the usual wait at the Chiswick flyover and it was mid-morning before they got to Ebury Street and his flat. She was wearing a lime green sweater and a white pleated skirt and she laughed because he couldn't even wait to close the door before he was pulling her to him. A few minutes later she was naked to the waist and his hands were fondling the smooth honey-coloured skin. His head was bent and his mouth was kissing her neck and shoulder and she felt his lust as he moved in excitement against her. Then as she responded his head came up slowly, and she bent back to let him see her breasts, and suddenly he said 'Christ Almighty'. She looked up quickly at his face and then turned to follow his stare.

From the small hall-way they looked into a sitting-room. Drawers had been pulled from cupboards and a desk, and letters and papers were strewn all over the floor. A small wall-safe was open, with its solid door hanging by one thick hinge. The marks of a gas torch spread on to the walls. Carpets had been pulled aside and alternate floor boards had been ripped up. A crow-bar still stood lodged between a floor board and a joist. Polystyrene foam was bursting from cuts in a settee and chairs. Books lay with their spines broken and pages adrift, and the phone had gone from its table, its trailing coiled lead disappeared behind an armchair that was lying on its side. The dead man lay with his head twisted to an impossible angle, one arm was outstretched and the other was bent beneath him. His legs trailed backwards from a chair and one suede shoe was half off his right foot although the lace was still tied tight.

The girl was very calm, and while Hallet phoned the police she put their bags in the bedroom and put on her sweater and brushed her hair. So far as he could see there was nothing missing, and the two plain clothes men had assured him that there was no need for any publicity.

27

Because of his status it was a Special Branch responsibility and that was that.

When the two plain clothes men were walking up Lower Belgrave Street one of them, Commander Bryant, said, 'Well I'll be interested to read the autopsy. It was Boris Suslov all right and we'll have to do an appreciation of why the GRU are interested in Hallet. I couldn't see any signs of how he was killed, probably a sternum thrust. The other interesting thing is what was he after and who knocked him off. I've got a feeling in my water that it would have been SIS. We'll notify them first and see what sort of reaction we get. We'd better check on the girl. He called her an assistant but I've never seen her around him before. Probably another one of his bits of crumpet. Hey – there's a taxi – give it a wave Joe.'

Hallet left the girl at the flat and took a taxi to his office suite near Sloane Square. He looked through a pile of letters and reports and made a few phone calls. His desk was a wide expanse of white Formica and at his left hand was a keyboard terminal that gave him access to his unit's IBM Series 370 computer, in the basement of the office block. He took out his diary, took down some figures and made a calculation. Then he walked over to the shelves of books and took down a copy of 'The Oxford Companion to English Literature' and turned to various pages as he referred to the figures on the paper. He ended up with a ten digit figure, and when he'd walked back to his desk he flipped the main switch on the terminal. A few seconds later he tapped out the figures on to the keyboard and then sat back and waited. The VDU that looked like a small TV screen, flickered and then held, so that the screen was pale blue. Figures fed in jerkily, digit by digit and line by line until the screen was full. Hallet tapped a key and the figures instantly became letters. Then slowly the letters cleared in groups of five until only ten remained. They were dotted about the screen but they read OMEGA MINUS, and then the screen was dark again. And Hallet knew that nobody had had access to his data bank whilst he'd been away.

He booked a suite for two nights at the Hilton and phoned his flat to arrange for the girl to meet him at the hotel. He had phoned his wife at the cottage in Worcester and after some pleasantries he had said he would be in London for the next three weeks. He didn't suggest that she join him and she didn't suggest it either. She had her horses and he had his girls and it was her opinion that she got the best of the deal.

After booking in he had walked her round the early evening streets. Through Shepherd Market into Curzon Street and then to Berkeley Square and Bond Street. They'd looked in Asprey's window and he'd seen a ring with a single diamond that would suit her long slim fingers. The ticket alongside the ring had said 'Acceptable gift – £1,500'. It wasn't so long ago when he would have laughed at the ridiculously coy description. But now that the money meant so little it wasn't worth a second thought. He'd have them send it around the next morning. As they walked arm in arm through the summer evening the gorgeous girl had turned heads and stopped traffic but she had eyes only for him, and he was flattered. Whether it was clothes, jewellery or money that would keep her happy he would supply it. He'd never had a girl like this and the beautiful face and the innocently erotic and compliant, eager body were the stuff that fantasies were made of.

They had dinner at Grosvenor House and walked back through the park and caught a taxi at Hyde Park Corner for the Festival Hall. He walked her along the Embankment and showed her the lights and the river. As they leaned against the stone parapet a River Police launch cruised by and the men must have seen her for they switched on their long-throw beam and swept it back and up to the parapet. For a few moments they were in the blazing light then it was silently doused, and with three blasts on the siren the launch sped on. Hallet didn't know that the signal was for 'Man overboard', and even if he had he would not have been amused. Like most adulterers he was a jealous man.

CHAPTER V

Sir John Walker was Director of Operations SIS and it is likely that only Ed Farrow would have considered it perfectly normal to invite him back for a night-cap to Cadogan Pier. They had dined at the Café Royal with their fellow members of the National Sporting Club and they had watched the boxing till it finished at eleven-fifteen. And now the embankment lights picked out the white shirts and the sheen on their dinner jackets as they stepped carefully down the wooden gangway to where the big Fjord swung on her moorings.

The MV *My Joanna* had been Ed Farrow's home for almost three years. She had twin 150 h.p. diesels and he could generally beat the weather in crossing the Channel. Although her hull and superstructure were heavy GRP, inside she was genuine teak and stainless steel. There wasn't the slightest spartan touch about *My Joanna*, she had every comfort a man on his own could want, and she could go 300 miles without re-fuelling.

Ed held back the canopy and switched on the cockpit lights and went down the companion-way into the saloon. A few minutes later Sir John was stretched out on one of the foam rubber seats with his head resting back against a bulkhead. His bow tie was undone and he was holding a malt whisky up to the light. 'My guess is Glen Livet, Ed.'

'Not bad for a gin drinker, actually it's Glen Fiddich but there's not much in it.'

Walker turned his turkey-cock face to Farrow and then looked down at his glass as he asked 'Any ideas on the Hallet business yet?'

'Well as you know I've only had a couple of days on it. The corpse has been identified as Boris Suslov, a Pole working for the GRU. He's not very important and he's been used mainly in the Middle East and Berlin so far. Seems to specialize in break-ins and theft of documents and that sort of thing. He was used by the Russians in the Portland spy ring, but only for photographing documents. I've put a complete set of tails on Hallet. Lots of people could be interested in what he's up to – including us. But there's no indication that he's doing anything special although I'm checking on that. The autopsy showed that the Pole died from a sudden blow that stopped the heart immediately.' He looked speculatively at Walker. 'Much the kind of stuff we got taught in the old days by the Shanghai policemen at Beaulieu, the heel of the hand under the sternum.'

Walker brushed his hand over his short grey hair. 'And who did it?'

Farrow laughed. 'I'd have said us,' and he looked quizzically across at his chief. Walker shook his head slowly, pursing his lips. 'No Ed, it's not us, and I wonder who else is interested in knocking off third-rate GRU men in London.'

'One thing that is interesting. Hallet was due back several days before he actually got back. The man had been there only three or four hours before Hallet found him. I'd have expected Hallet's place to be gone over when it was perfectly safe, some days earlier. Hallet didn't book his flight till the day before, but he was well past his scheduled return date. I'd guess he was overdue because he was coaxing this girl into coming with him.'

Walker put down his glass and stood up. He had to stoop slightly as the boat only had 6-foot headroom. Hands in pockets and gently rocking on his heels, he said 'It's a bloody scandal that a man like Hallet can get away with this third-rate behaviour. All those little girls and the near rapes and the covering up. Stupid bastard ought to have had it cut off years ago. A brain like that and the morals of a Soho ponce.'

Farrow walked back with his chief and they stood talking for a few moments before waving to a taxi.

Back at the boat he checked the warps for the night and then went on board, zipping the canopy behind him. It was one of his pleasures, the time on his own in the bright neat saloon. The smooth, oiled teak of the saloon table and the bulkheads, the sparseness and masculinity

31

and the incongruity of stepping out of evening dress on a boat.

He could see the outline of the bridge across the Thames and hear the distant noise of cars and buses on the embankment. Lying on his back he picked up Reed's *Nautical Almanac* from the side table and roughed out a trip to Guernsey. But Reed's was too heavy and his eyes were closing, so he called it a day. As the fog of sleep swirled towards him he thought of something Walker had said that rang a bell, but it faded into thoughts of the channel tides at Dover, and then he was asleep.

Sergei Venturi gave additional orders to the Red Army sergeant outside his office door, then turned the key, and after testing the door he put the key in his jacket pocket. When he got to the ground floor he stood at the entrance to the cloister-like arcade. A group of girls giggled, thinking he was looking them over, and he was indeed looking intently in their direction. But he saw no girls. He was trying to think why he was standing there or where he was going. He was dog-tired and it felt as if his brain was too big for his head. His mind was like a starter-motor when the batteries were almost flat – it groaned. He felt in his pocket for a clue and then there was a man in official service uniform taking his brief-case and bags, and the man said 'The car's at the main entrance, comrade colonel', and then he remembered. He was on his way to Moscow and there was a morning meeting tomorrow.

At the airfield the car went straight to the helicopter take-off pad. There was a little MI-2 with its rotors turning jerkily, and as he stepped up the short aluminium ladder he saw that the only other passengers were a heavily bandaged man on a stretcher, a young woman in a heavy fur coat and a man who was obviously a doctor. There was a saline drip on a short stand and as the helicopter started its climb the doctor held it steady and checked the feed-line. Nobody spoke during the whole of the journey to Moscow and Venturi felt depressed and dispirited as his baggage was loaded into the big car which drew up alongside the aircraft. A small yellow ambulance with a flashing light was waiting for the others.

32

He looked out from the car into the darkness. There were lights in the new blocks that straggled along the road, but it all looked dreary and grim. Sooner than he expected they were at the Moscow ring-road and twenty minutes later he was in the official apartment in Dzerzhinski Square. There was a note saying that the meeting had been postponed until 1400 hours. Despite his tiredness there was something about Moscow that livened him up. His head still ached but the fog in his mind was clearing. He set out the chess board and leafed through the newly published record of the Spassky–Fischer games in Reykjavik. He settled on the third game and made careful notes as he made the opening moves.

The room was ornate and old-fashioned but it had a certain taste, an importance that couldn't be denied. It would be difficult to be gay or flippant in such a room, it was made for serious discussion and Venturi had realized from the start that the mere choosing of this particular room and these particular men was an indication that he was being subjected to pressure. But his reputation and background ensured that it was a hint and not a threat. The discussions had taken over two hours and the room was full of smoke, the responsibility of one man. The man tapped the bending cigar ash against a silver tray and, with head bent, tried to work out how to voice his conclusions without giving offence. Nobody would have accused Boris Sarkisov of being a diplomat. As a deputy minister he had no need to be diplomatic but he liked this young man Venturi and they had given him a beating for two hours. He'd given back blow for blow but they had reached an impasse and it was time to break the log-jam. Finally he looked up, looked around the table and from habit looked up at the beautifully decorated ceiling. Directly in his line of sight was an angel with arms and legs spread-eagled. The angel was a beautiful brunette and Sarkisov suspected that he was probably the only man who thought the flying angel had a sexy face and that her youthful limbs were spread in invitation. Then, as so often, the words he sought came to him.

'You've done an enormous amount of research on this

33

business comrade Venturi, and our colleagues here today will appreciate its value. But the fact of the matter is, that although we now know a hell of a lot about Hallet, we don't know what he is up to. Yet we've had a reliable tip that he's up to something. Yes comrade – speak up.'

'We have not been told where this tip came from.'

'True.'

'Is there any reason why this small committee should not know the source?'

Sarkisov looked down at the green baize covering the table then again up at the ceiling. He whistled silently for a few moments as the others watched his face. Finally his head came up and he looked across at Venturi.

'It was a KGB source, completely reliable. I can't say more than that. It wouldn't help anyway.'

He sensed that Venturi or one of the others might press him further so he didn't wait for comment but went on, 'I think you'd do better to put together a team and go over. You could have number two apparat in London.'

His piggy eyes saw the protest on Venturi's face and his mouth open to protest. He put up his hand. 'You would take over as controller with all necessary resources.' He paused, and looked sternly at Venturi. 'We've got to nail this down quickly and I'm not wasting any more time.' He stood up and looked around the table. 'Everyone agreed?'

Nobody spoke and he looked again at Venturi.

'Agreed then, gentlemen – and you comrade?' Venturi nodded briefly and half smiled. 'Yes, comrade minister – agreed.'

CHAPTER VI

The man in the pale blue suit was standing reading the plaque at the Rockefeller Center and then he turned his back and faced the shops. He walked slowly over to the novelty shop, looked in the window, and then looked at the steps to the door. On the second step he saw it. A crude outline of a fish in red chalk. As he turned away he smiled. He remembered the Pole telling him that the fish had been used in the Roman Empire as an underground sign for the Christians. They had found fish signs in the catacombs of Rome.

The fish on the step was without eyes so it meant a long drag over to the cinema at the back of Times Square. He paid for a ticket and saw that it was a re-run of Spencer Tracy and Katherine Hepburn in *Guess Who's Coming to Dinner?* He watched it for about twenty minutes and then made his way to the toilets. The place stank of stale urine and the floor was filthy. He opened the right hand door and saw with a shock that the cistern had been torn from the wall and it hung now, held only by the twisted lead pipe. The lid was smashed and lay on the filthy floor in pieces, but by some miracle the ball valve still operated and there was the cylinder taped with insulating tape, under the valve and above the water line. He pulled at it and it came away easily. He peeled off the tape and flushed it down the adjoining toilet. The aluminium cylinder he slid in his pocket. He went through the emergency doors and came out at the back of the cinema. The small cylinder was in the Polish embassy's diplomatic bag to Warsaw the next day. It contained three days' Samos photographs of the Soviet Union, two days covering China and a short strip covering Great Britain from a line above St. Albans for the nights of 23, 24 and 25 July.

A girl who worked in the main CIA complex paid

$1,500, that day, off her mortgage on a well-built but small ranch-style house outside San Diego. She couldn't put it in the bank because God knows how many organizations got access to bank accounts these days. She'd worked in CIA for nine years and she'd been selling out to the Russians for the whole of that time. She'd laid down the going rate right at the start and the Russians had agreed without demur. She was ideal for what they wanted. In the right place, with security clearance and a grim determination to wreak her revenge for what had been done to her. What had been done she would have difficulty in telling but it was probably most vividly held in her mind by a picture of a broken-down truck. Her family were wandering fruit-pickers and even in 1939 they'd been hounded from town to town, desperately poor and permanently hungry. She'd remembered the truck breaking down and her father looking up as he worked on a broken leaf spring. He said slowly, looking up at her mother, 'Ma, I can't stand up. I'm done for.' And he'd died. She remembered the Highway Patrol man standing at the dusty roadside. He was eating from a bunch of grapes and he touched her father's leg with his boot. 'You can't leave a cadaver lying around the road. It's agin the law.' He'd had one last mouthful of grapes and tossed the rest into the field. He'd put his leg over his motor-cycle and had ridden off with easy competent style. She had been four and she remembered the silence when the man had gone. And she'd remembered the look on her mother's face. The orphanage had paid for her secretarial training and she'd never looked back.

James Hallet sat comfortably in his office with his feet up on his desk. His companion, who was sitting more formally on the other side of the desk, was operating a small electronic calculator and referring to figures in a file. Sir Martin Mace was probably the ablest money man in the City of London, and he and Hallet had been friends from the time when Sir Martin administered a small trust that had enabled Hallet to have time to think, the time and the thinking from which his plastic conducting material had emerged. Sir Martin was a jolly man who treated money with no more reverence than he did nuts and bolts. He set no store by reverence, but he could turn £5,000 into £25,000 in a couple of months. With lesser amounts he was hopeless and with greater amounts he was a genius. He put the calculator aside and leaned back smiling at Hallet. 'Like I said James – near enough 27 million as of last Tuesday.'

'Pounds or dollars?'

'Oh pounds, but it's not in pounds of course. I've got it in marks, Swiss francs, yen, pounds, dollars, and what have you. It's too big an amount to fluctuate very much.'

Hallet put his hands behind his head and stretched out comfortably. As if they hadn't just been talking he said, 'You know, Martin, the thing that really used to bug me before you fixed me up with the Ryland Trust was that nobody – trustees, commerce, industry, the government – nobody would give me time to think. In this bloody country they don't think you're working unless you're scribbling on paper or talking on the telephone. Sit back comfortably and think, and they get uneasy. You can be writing crap or talking crap – doesn't matter, at least they can see you doing it – but they're never sure you really *are* thinking. There's nothing to show and it worries the poor sods no end. You know, Sir bloody William at the Ministry had put in three recommendations for my removal, for lack of effort mind you, in the three months before I published the news of the plastic conductor. Thank God it was listed in my contract as personal prior work.' He turned to Mace, banging his fist on the desk for emphasis. 'Do you know Martin, that took me ten minutes at the outside, that bloody plastic. Ten minutes. There was a buckshee atom in the conductivity pattern, always this useless atom. That's what conductivity is really about, Martin, and you can structure that bloody spare in certain polymers.' He slapped his hand on the desk. 'All you need is time to think and a nice big data bank.'

'So why've you dragged me over here now? I've heard it all before Jim. Your money's always going to be much the same unless you have new licensees and then it will increase. Anyway you've never worried about the cash before. What's on your mind?'

37

Hallet swung down his legs from the desk and stood up slowly. Hands in pockets and looking at the carpet he walked up and down behind the desk and in front of the big windows. Then he started speaking, as if he was trying to be precise with his words. 'Martin I'm trying to make up my mind what to do. Three months ago I came across something – just thinking again – and it has no commercial or industrial applications – or at least they'd be very limited and specialized. But – and I must emphasize this – as a weapon of war it would be devastating. Oddly enough it doesn't kill people – not directly anyway – but it could bring a town, a city, a whole country to a complete standstill. It could push them back into the dark ages by steps.' His head jerked up and he looked at Mace. 'This is not surmise Martin, it's fact. And in the tiniest possible way I've actually done it – it worked – bang on. Whichever government had this could force the others to do whatever it wanted – it sounds ridiculous and dramatic but I swear it's true.' He swung round at the end of his path. 'So what do I do Martin?'

'Give it to this country.'

'Oh for Christ's sake, Martin, just think of it – the bloody Establishment – the committees – the Authorities for this that and the other. No Martin, we've suffered enough under these stupid bastards.'

'Who've you got in mind – the Russians?'

Hallet sighed. 'No, not them either. In fact that's the bloody problem, there isn't any government I'd give it to. Not one.'

'Fair enough. Well why not just forget it then?'

'You couldn't do that Martin. First of all somebody'll drop on it one of these days. Could be tomorrow, could be a couple of hundred years. It's not an area where you'd do research. There's no pay-off. Except for destruction. But apart from that there's a second reason. I was stupid. I gave myself a private "demo" and it left a lot of clues. I think various people could try putting them together. They won't succeed but they'll establish that there's something, and they'll connect me with it.'

'Sounds dangerous.'

'Yes, I think it is in a way.'

'What do you want me to do?'

'Well, one thing I want you to do is to pay suitable amounts of money to various people and it mustn't be traceable to me.'

'Who are they?'

'Their names and addresses are on this sheet. They are people who were damaged by my one experiment. The only one that isn't there is an American, the pilot of an FE-111E that crashed in Northumberland on the night of 25 July. You'll trace him through their embassy, but I couldn't do it. The little radio fellow, I'd like the payment to cover the house as well as compensation. The deck hand on HMS *Pillager* has no family so maybe Barnardo's who brought him up would do. Be generous, it was my fault, and it was irresponsible. But I actually learned something.'

Sir Martin took the sheet of paper and folded it up and pushed it in his pocket without reading it. 'You want a drink, Jim?'

Hallet shook his head and grinned, 'No chum I'm heading home.'

'I hear she's an absolute corker.'

'Who said so?'

'Oh about forty or so chaps who've seen her with you.'

'They jealous?'

'Too bloody true they're jealous.'

Hallet walked with Mace to the lift and held his hand against the door when it opened. 'Martin if you have a view about the problem in the next couple of days, let me know.'

'I will Jim. So long.'

The fighter was doing 1,800 m.p.h. It was a neat little SUKHOI Su-lla with two Lyolka AL-9 reheating turbos, and half-way between Moscow and Berlin the pilot spoke on the intercom to Venturi. 'You'll be changing to a small plane in Berlin comrade.' Then they were approaching the airfield. They'd taken less than an hour.

At Berlin they changed to a Cessna, a non-pressurized 310 and they flew low and long on a flight plan that ended at Cherbourg. But they went out over the Channel well east of Cherbourg and as they flew back low over the coast they followed the railway out of Barfleur for three or four miles and then there was a twenty-acre field with its stubble still smoking where the aftermath from the harvest had been fired. They landed easily but bumpily in the fields to the west. There was a 'deux chevaux' waiting for them at the gate to the lane and half an hour later they pulled up at the quay in Barfleur. The little harbour held two fishing vessels and a solitary dinghy. An inflatable with an outboard took Venturi and his guide to a white motor-cruiser which was anchored outside the harbour north-west of the beacon. There was no name on her transom. She was about 32 feet overall and she had twin Perkins diesels which were trailing a little blue smoke as they idled. A pale-faced man reached over for Venturi's five bags and they were stowed in the cockpit and covered with light canvas.

There was a blow from the north-east and the boat pulled to port against her anchor. All Venturi's seamanship cried out to put another anchor down, but he just watched and said nothing.

Ten minutes later the two men, the captain and his single crew, were heaving at the anchor warp, and as the wind dropped for a moment the boat backed slightly and the anchor came up from about two fathoms. The captain brought her head round to starboard and she bucked slightly as she met the tide across to the main channel. Venturi looked back over the stern and he could see the square tower of the church. Then the boat's head came back to port and Venturi looked at the small compass on his wristband and estimated that they had settled on a course of about 40 degrees true and they were making about 13 knots against a 3-knot current.

Venturi had heard the men talking and guessed they must be Irish. He stood by the crewman who was steering and the boat came round to port again and now they were heading due north. He saw a metal sign over the chart table and it said 'Project 31 Series II made by Marine Projects, Plymouth, Devon'. The captain came up the companionway with a mug of tea and Venturi sat in the comfortable navigator's seat and slowly sipped the sweet hot liquid. 'My God,' he thought, 'what savages who drink
40

such muck.' They made steady progress and Venturi went below and slept for two hours on the forward bunks.

When Venturi went back up into the wheelhouse the captain was resting his elbows on the upper chart table and looking through a pair of binoculars at the coast that could just be seen ahead. They were still making good speed and half an hour later they were standing off a sandy shore with a low profile but no visible habitation of any kind. The engines idled and were spasmodically revved to keep the boat's head into the wind. Then with a streaming wake and a large bow wave a white launch came from a hidden creek. She fetched up alongside with a flourish and the roar of twin engines in reverse. Venturi, ex-Red Navy, was amused. It had style but was bad seamanship – and he realized the boats were identical. The other crew had put out fenders and the boats stood alongside and rode the swell together. The captain from Venturi's boat stepped across to the other cockpit and down the hatchway. A few minutes later another man crossed over to Venturi's boat and took command at the wheel. He was a young man, brown and weatherbeaten. The other boat had her name in blue on her bows and across her transom: *Blue Star* registered Port of London. They must have been on white plastic for with a sharp order to the crew the lines were released, and as they slowly drifted away from the other boat he saw they were ripping off her name at the bows and on the stern. Then they were tossed into the cockpit of Venturi's boat. The young man turned to him and said, 'Good day to you mister. They're going on round to Ramsgate so's they'll get noticed. This boat notified the coastguard that it was heading for Ramsgate. They've just come from the yacht basin. Supposed to be trying her engines. We shall go back in like, and take up a berth there, and that way they'll think we've only been out for an hour and a bit. We'll just 'old on till the other boys are away now.' And the crew were carefully fixing the plastic names to the bows and stern.

'Where exactly is this?'

The young man looked round. 'This be Chichester mister and we're gonna drop you in the yacht basin moorings. There's well nigh 700 boats in there right now so they

41

won't be noticing us too much. And if they do, well so much the better like. Now I'll have to be watching mister, there's a nasty old bar ahead of us at the entrance. It's a right devil with a southerly blow but we'll be nicely over it if we's careful.'

They went east on a half flood up the channel. After another half-hour the captain said without turning his head, 'That's Itchenor over there on the starboard side and then there's about another mile to the basin. We've got to go through the lock there so I'd like you to go below and keep out of sight. I don't suppose they'll remember anyone but me but we don't want to take any risks, do we?'

Forty minutes later they were neatly tied up at a finger pontoon, the engines silent and just a gentle slap of water against the smooth hull. The captain went off and strolled back with another man ten minutes later. They stood on the pontoon alongside the boat and smoked and talked. Then they both came aboard.

The other man introduced himself. 'My name's O'Reilly, Allen O'Reilly. I was expecting you. If you've no objection I'd like you to stay here for a couple of days on the boat. We're buying you a house just outside London. It should be completed tomorrow. I'd like an extra day or two.'

Venturi took over the boat as if it were his own. The bilges were pumped out, decks mopped down and polished, metalwork cleaned and polished and in the early afternoon Venturi was re-splicing and whipping the bights on the nylon ropes. He was burning the frayed ends of a rope when a shadow fell across him. He looked up slowly and it was O'Reilly with a small, blue, plastic, Pan-Am bag. O'Reilly stepped down on to the seat and then to the cockpit gratings. He sat down and lit a cigarette. Then he fiddled in the plastic bag and lifted out a brown envelope. 'I've got you a passport mister. It's an Irish one but it's genuine.' He smiled across at Venturi. 'We've done the IRA a few good turns and we asked for a bit of help from them.' Then he handed over various items. 'We've kept to the name we were told – Stanley Vigo. We've opened a bank account in your name at Barclays in Croydon. So here's a cheque book and a Barclaycard. Here's a driving

42

licence. We've bought you a second-hand MG. The house will be ready in two days, it's in a suburb south of London called Sanderstead and I've got the maps here to show you.'

Venturi had had two previous periods in England. There'd been a six months' English course at one of the London polytechnics with a Finnish passport and cover story, and a two months' stint with a Soviet buying mission. During his time with the mission he'd had a cover name and there'd been no side activities. They wanted him to get up to date again in the language.

Finally O'Reilly brought out a sealed package. 'That's from the Polish embassy. I'd like you to have been identified down here. Do you know anything about boats?'

Venturi laughed. 'Not too much Mr. O'Reilly, but enough.'

'Well, let's go along to Saltern's the boat brokers here at the yacht basin.'

Venturi and Saltern's directors were almost equally enthusiastic about a motor-sailer made in Essex under the trade name Salar. He went on board the demonstration model and they were impressed with his inspection.

On the evening of the third day his gear was piled into the MG, and he drove off following O'Reilly's spoken instructions. Two hours later they were in the drive-way of a detached house in Sanderstead.

The house in Sanderstead matched Venturi's cover as a photographer. A new wing had been built into the garden by a previous owner, with a large studio and dark-room incorporated. The studio was complete with lights, electronic flash, and Linhof and Hasselblad cameras. It was good cover for the visitors who would be coming at all hours of the day and night. In the darkroom they fixed a transceiver that operated just above the ten-metre band and could receive and transmit between anywhere in England and Moscow, or Leningrad for that matter. He could use ultra speed Morse in a five-group code and a ten-minute transmission could be reduced to 2·5 seconds.

After two weeks Venturi felt he fitted in well enough with the middle-class suburb. He had all his Leningrad material on microfilm, and any of it could be blown-up for examination or photographing in a matter of minutes.

43

O'Reilly had faded out of the picture and Venturi was now using the experienced GRU apparat that had been operating in the UK for nine years.

Every day reports came in from the team who were checking on Hallet. They had tried and failed to gain access to his office. There had been four attempts and at the last one they had been prepared to use force to get through the outer door. The oxy-acetylene torch had been played on the surface for less than three seconds when all the lights came on, and they were only just clear of the building before two cars full of police emptied in the forecourt and the men surrounded the block. They saw Hallet come twenty minutes later. He was in evening dress and they saw him pull keys from his pocket as he walked briskly into the main entrance. It looked like even the police hadn't been able to get in.

The pleasant warning gong rang softly and the attendant took the ticket from Hallet and led him down the short corridor and they settled quickly into the box. The auditorium lights were lowered and George Solti walked on to rapturous applause and from the other side came Tortelier weaving his 'cello round the first violins. The big leonine head bent over the 'cello for a moment, then the bow was ready and his head came up, and Solti was into the Elgar 'cello concerto. It was an all Elgar night, a rare indulgence for the Festival Hall but commercially astute, as the almost full house indicated.

Farrow stood in deep shadow against the back wall of the empty Royal Box and he kept the small binoculars on Hallet's face. He looked too at the girl. She was exceptionally pretty and Farrow could see why Hallet was so involved. Most men would have been flattered to be seen with such a youthful beauty. They had gleaned surprisingly little information about her. She was travelling on a Danish passport and her address given to Immigration was Hallet's and a house in Ny Vestergade. She had made few journeys from the flat on her own and they had been simple shopping expeditions to Jaeger, Mary Davies in Queen Street and a shoe shop in Bond Street. They had put a routine request to the CIA but that had drawn a blank except for

44

the address she had given of her relatives on Lexington.

The concert ended. They hadn't dared to emulate the last night of the Proms and they'd brought the proceedings to an end with the 'Wand of Youth' suite. Farrow had seen Hallet hand in hand with the girl walking back to the Festival Hall car-park. They'd kissed at the side of the Lamborghini, got into the car, and then roared round the Waterloo Station island, over Westminster Bridge and had finally parked the car off Belgrave Square and walked back to Ebury Street and the flat.

An hour later they had almost finished a game of Scrabble, the girl sitting opposite to Hallet in a new, green leather armchair. There was a cassette of Viennese songs on the hi-fi and it got to the closing bars of a lush variation of *'Sag' beim Abschied leise Servus'* and the girl said 'Play that again for me Jimmy, I love that much.' He laughed, 'Miss Kristina Olsen you have excellent bad taste – a sure liking for schmalz.' She grinned back. 'Yes, you right. So I have it again, yes.' He nodded. 'Provided you do it. Just press the red button and it'll automatically turn itself back to the beginning again.' She stood up and he watched her as she walked to the tape-deck, pressed the button and watched the cassette re-wind. The light from the standard lamp shone on her back and she was naked and beautiful. Even without the sex she was beautiful. Like a baby or a boat or a smooth stone on a beach. But she wasn't without the sex and he called out to her 'Turn round and let me look at you.' She tossed her head. 'Is nearly done here then I show you me.' Then there were lots of strings and a harp, and a piano played the orchestra into *'Drunt in der Lobau, hab' ich ein Mädl geküsst . . .'* and she turned, and smiled as she stood there, unembarrassed and natural, as he looked at her. Still smiling she walked over and stood in front of him, and the red warning light on the hi-fi had glowed all night through till morning.

CHAPTER VII

The reports of payments to the wife of the RAF Wing
Commander killed in the FE-111E crash, to George Sharp's
sister and the Barnardo's home that had cared for Ordinary
Seaman Fordyce slowly filtered back to Ed Farrow. Sir
Martin Mace had arranged for the payments to be made
through a small insurance company, a subsidiary of a
merchant bank owned by one of his clients. Only the murder
of the RAF Sergeant at Boulmer had triggered the inten-
sive and continuous interest in everything unusual that happened in the northern half of the county of Northumberland.

Except that all the deaths apart from the murder had
occurred on the same night and within fifty miles or so of
each other there seemed to be no link between the four
events. There seemed to be no link except in one case,
with RAF Boulmer. But that exception had a distant connection to Hallet. Hallet had been commissioned by the
Ministry of Defence to examine, and if possible improve, a
telemetry device for precise measurement of the position
of ships and aircraft from fixed points. Not only their
bearings but their distance down the bearing. Prior to
Hallet the device had been accurate to just under half a
mile. After Hallet had done his redesign it had been accurate to six inches. The first practical test of the new
apparatus was on the night of 24 July and Hallet had been
invited up to Boulmer to watch a gunnery test on a towed
target raft. He had arrived four days earlier and had taken
over one of the Marconi stores buildings as his quarters
and workshop. The Royal Navy had co-operated for the
benefit of the RAF boffins at Boulmer and HMS *Pillager*,
a squat little Admiralty tug, had bullocked her way up the
North Sea crewed by the Royal Marine Auxiliary Service.

The first shot fired at the towed raft had been right on
target but, on instruction from the Wing Commander in
charge of the test, the skipper of the *Pillager* had sent a
deck-hand to examine the hit and note the instrument

46

readings before the next shot, and he had hardly landed on the raft with its maze of measuring instruments when the raft had seemed to explode in a blaze of bright light. As the heavy structure plummeted beneath the waves the skipper had ordered the towing hawser to be released and the raft had sunk to the bottom of the North Sea. It was far too deep to be salvaged. The report on the incident had indicated that Dr Hallet had appeared to be disturbed by what had happened and, despite the fact that the explosion or fire could have no connection with his redesigned measuring instrument, he reacted for an hour as if he were in some way responsible. In the early hours of the morning the MO had given Hallet a sedative to allow him to sleep, as he appeared to be still disturbed.

Farrow decided that there was so little material to work on that even this report warranted further investigation. He'd taken the boat up-river to the Westland heliport and shortly after he had made her fast, he heard and felt the rackety clatter of a Royal Navy Westland Lynx. The helicopter took them low across East Anglia and then the pilot followed the coastline up to Tynemouth. They had been instructed not to land at RAF Boulmer because of interference with their instruments, and arrangements had been made for them to land at a farm near Embleton. A car was waiting to take them to the RAF station.

All day Farrow talked with officers and men who'd come into contact with Hallet, and all that he could establish was that Hallet had been engrossed in the preparations for the test and had spent most of the time working in his own quarters. He had been quietly pleased when the test was successful first time, and then deflated when he'd heard of the death of the deck-hand. But that was normal enough, others had been upset by the tragedy too. Three hours after the test the news had come in about the FE-111E. Hallet had been in the Mess with some of the technical officers and when he'd heard the news of the crash he had sat for a moment or two, then got up and walked to his quarters. The CO hadn't liked the look on his face and had told the Medical Officer to check on his condition. At a unit like Boulmer all specialists were top grade and that applied to the MO as much as anybody. Squadron Leader

47

Waring had grey hair and he'd been around the services for a long time.

'Could you just go over exactly what happened after the CO asked you to have a look at Dr. Hallet?'

'Well now. I came back here to the surgery and picked up my little black bag.'

'Any reason why you should do that?'

'Just routine, colonel. I knocked on Hallet's door and got no reply so I walked in. Hallet was sitting on the bunk bed with his face in his hands and he didn't hear me come in. He appeared to be in a state of nervous exhaustion. I walked over and put my hand on his shoulder and spoke his name and he looked up. Seemed surprised, or maybe confused is more like it. I asked him what was wrong and he said nothing was wrong. I checked his pulse and temperature. Slightly abnormal both of them but no more than shock or exhaustion would cause. I told him I was concerned that he should get a good night's sleep and I gave him a shot of morphine and laid him back on his bunk, made him comfortable, and I sat with him till he was sleeping. Next day I checked him and he was quite normal but a bit drowsy from the morphine.'

'Did he talk at all? Did he respond in any way?'

'No, but that's quite normal with shock or exhaustion.'

'Any particular reason why you sat with him until he was asleep?'

'I suppose there was really. Probably a touch of the Florence Nightingales. He looked oddly vulnerable, rather young in a way. Looked like he needed some reassurance.'

'Did you say anything to him at that time?'

'Nothing beyond the usual noises to patients who are about to succumb to morphine.'

'Did he say anything?'

'Let me think now. He said the usual thing like "It's beginning to work doc", and so on. He asked what day it was and I told him, yes – I remember now – he said something like "Must have been the reciprocal" and then his eyes were closed.'

'Any significance to you in what he said?'

'Not to me, I've heard it too many times from navigators who've pranged or got into trouble from laying off a wrong course. They shunt the pilot off on a course and then find they've made a bog of the calculation and sent him in the opposite direction – down the reciprocal. Zero degrees north instead of 180 degrees or due south. Happens to the best of them but nobody gets used to it.'

And that had been all. The helicopter had flown up the Thames from Southend and they'd landed at Battersea just as the light was going. He'd invited the pilot on board *My Joanna* for a drink, and then he'd had a meal and turned in.

The telephone rang on *My Joanna* just after 4 a.m. Farrow rubbed his eyes and walked to the saloon table, picked up the phone and said 'Nine seven nine.'

'That Ed Farrow?'

'Yes. Who's that?'

'Tad Anders, Ed. Sorry to phone at this time but I'm doing a stint in Central Intelligence and I've just realized that a bit of my jigsaw fits a bit of yours. At least I think it does. When can we meet?'

'Is it about Hallet?'

'Yes and it looks like the GRU are tailing him.'

'Let's meet right now then. I doubt if I'll get a taxi this time of night, or morning rather, how about you come over to the boat.'

'Where is it?'

'At the heliport at Battersea.'

'I'll be there in about half an hour.'

Anders was another of SIS's old hands and he and Farrow had been friends for many years. Not an intense friendship but an enduring one and they had often co-operated, always without friction. Half English, half Polish, Anders was shrewd, experienced and tough. Farrow was dressed and waiting when the car lights swept over the heliport and then were doused. A few moments later Anders was on board and they were sitting at the teak table in the saloon.

'I've got a whole pile of reports here Ed. I put my chaps on to a routine check of Hallet when a lowgrade GRU man was knocked off in Hallet's flat. You'll find that the GRU

49

have been keeping a watch on Hallet and we've got reliable information that there's a top GRU operator over here because of Hallet. You'll find two Joint Intelligence evaluations of the situation and their conclusion is that the GRU have had some sort of indication that Hallet is on to something of importance. What's the state of the game with you?' Farrow brought him up to date.

'My feeling Ed, is that there's a major piece missing and it's my experience that once we get this far it kind of sets off the clockwork and the pieces start dropping into place. Can we agree to make it a joint operation under your control? Until it begins to sort itself out anyway.'

Farrow had agreed and after Anders had gone he read through the reports carefully but they didn't add much to the picture except that the Russians were interested in Hallet too.

As Anders had forecast, the missing piece or a major single piece, was put into the machinery later that day.

Nobody was kept waiting at 11 Downing Street and certainly not an old friend like Sir Martin Mace. The Chancellor had known him from the days when they both felt outcasts at an over-extrovert prep school in Sussex.

'Hello Martin. Good to see you. How's Martha and the family?'

'Everybody's fine, Dickie, thank you. And how about your brood?'

'All in good form so far as I know. I don't get much time now of course. I've put aside an hour so we can relax while you dish me all the dirt about your Throgmorton Street friends. Make yourself comfortable do.'

'Dickie it's not about the City that I've come. It's about Hallet.'

'I see. And what's friend Hallet up to? I hear he's got another young girl in tow. Something of a beauty by all accounts.'

'Yes. I've only met her once and she's quite a dish. But that's not the problem of course. I don't really know how to go about this Dickie. It's not really a financial matter at all. It's probably a security matter. Hallet is not only a
50

good friend of mine, he's a client as well and what I'm doing is unprofessional and slightly offensive. I don't like it at all. Now I know you and trust you. I don't want trouble for Hallet but I'm worried about something. Can we talk or not?'

The Chancellor raised a quizzical eyebrow and looked across at his old friend. 'You know, Martin, security isn't part of my province at all. Wouldn't it be wiser for me to get one of the security chaps in? I'll stay too, of course.'

'I couldn't do that Dickie. I really couldn't. I'd rather push off and let it all happen if it's going to happen. I'm already interfering. I suspect I'm betraying a confidence and I want to get it off my mind without feeling too guilty.'

'All right then Martin. Let's have it. But I must warn you that if security is really involved I would be bound to put the matter in the right hands. Without mentioning the source of course.' He leaned back and obviously gave all his attention to Sir Martin Mace, financier.

'Hallet has told me that he's devised, or come upon, something that could put the nation possessing it in a position to dominate the rest of the world.' He paused waiting for a reaction but the Chancellor didn't even blink. He'd heard too many tales about ultimate weapons, death rays and bugs that spelt the end of the world, and he didn't believe a word of it. Amazing how astute financiers like Martin could be carried away by scientists. They never seemed to learn. But no shade of disbelief crossed his listening face and Sir Martin continued. 'He told me in absolute confidence and asked if I could suggest a solution. You may know that a man was found dead in Hallet's flat the day he returned from the States. I gather that there's the possibility he was a Russian or a Pole.' He'd said enough, he felt, to arouse some interest and he was not saying more until he'd got some response.

The Chancellor took a deep breath. The news about the Pole or whatever, did make a difference but he was not sure how much.

'You know, Martin, since I've been in senior office I've had my share of finding committees and teams to finalize the new secret weapon. I find that if it's initiated by the services it's out of date long before it's in service and if

51

it's initiated by scientists it never quite makes it. They're always nearly there and another hundred thousand would buy finality. But it never does. We end up buying the American version or doing a phony "joint" deal with the French. So don't expect me to leap about at the drop of an ultimate weapon. However, I have to face the fact that you are sufficiently impressed to come and tell me about it.

'Suffice it to say that that won't be forgotten and I shall mention it to the PM. So tell me what was your suggestion to Hallet?'

'At the time, I suggested he handed it over to the Government and he wasn't having any. As you know he's not an Establishment man.'

The Chancellor nodded. 'Of course not. These bloody scientists think the whole world is dependent on them. They talk of humanity but you wouldn't catch them down where the muck is – they impugn everybody else's motives but they fight as dirty a fight for an extra few quid as the next man.' The Chancellor was losing his cool and Sir Martin waited silently.

'Well now Martin, let's get back to the practical aspects. I'll have to have a word with the bloodhounds. I'll be very discreet of course. And in the meantime I suggest you keep me informed if you get any idea of what it's all about. Now tell me why Walford really backed out of the merger with Main's, there seemed no . . .'

And they were back to more dramatic things.

Sir Martin Mace's conversation with the Chancellor had filtered through to Farrow and at last the picture had a frame. There was a lot of picture missing but there was a centre to the operation now.

The saddles creaked with the sound of expensive leather that had lasted long and had been well cared for. Both horses were walking easily but there was foam at their mouths and their necks shone with sweat. The autumn morning was just sharp enough for breath to condense in small clouds. Their knees touched as the horses were momentarily out of step, and Hallet reined in the chestnut and reached over and laid his hand on the grey's neck, slowing her to a halt. The beech trees were gold and red and already the leaves were swirling slowly down. Hallet looked across at the girl affectionately. 'You know you give me great peace Kristina. You don't ask about my work or money or quiz me about my family. You don't cash in on my feeling for you.' She turned at her hips and her hand went up to the black riding cap. 'Why should I Jimmy? We are both happy and nothing else matters, does it?'

He took off his cap and smoothed his hand inside it, stretching it gently. He flipped it back on his head again and said, 'Thanks for staying with me.' For a moment she thought he was going to say something more but he smiled and pulled back his heels and both horses moved off. At Hyde Park Corner they waited for the help of a policeman. They had breakfast at Grosvenor House and were back at the flat by eleven.

There was post on the floor in the hallway. He stood tearing open the envelopes and glancing at the contents. One he passed over to the girl without comment. It was an invitation to the Polish embassy to meet a group of visiting scientists. 'How about your coming with me?'

'Will be very nice Jimmy.'

He laughed. 'It'll be a grinding bore – but not if you're with me.'

Farrow decided that it was time he checked on what the Russians knew.

On the wall of the studio at Sanderstead were several dozen photographs of Hallet and several of Hallet and the girl. There was a photograph of Hallet's flat from the outside and some poorish shots of the interior. There were photographs of the block housing Hallet's office suite and an architect's plan of the building itself. There was a good aerial view of Boulmer. There were typed time-tables of Hallet's movements. There were extracts from records at Company's House, of companies with which Hallet had connections. There were the patent specifications for 'Plasticond' from which he'd made his fortune.

Venturi had just come back from a trip to London. He'd

had a quiet inspection of his troops and early on he'd realized that there was another tail on Hallet apart from his team of two. One of his people was processing the photographs of the tail in the dark room.

There had been further information from Moscow confirming their opinion, and the opinion of other reliable sources, that Hallet was up to something important. There was no indication of what he might be up to. He had asked for the source of the information on two occasions and in neither case did he receive a reply.

'Perhaps you'd call a taxi for me.'

'Oh there's no need for that James, I can take you in the Mini.'

He looked up at her as she stood near the window nervously rearranging a bowl of flowers. She hadn't been surprised at his request for a divorce and she hadn't shown any resistance. She hadn't asked about money, although he'd talked about it himself. She was still the girl from the tennis club and the stables. A Thelwell girl grown up. Inoffensive, unassuming and consistent. There were many men who would be after Laura Hallet and they wouldn't all be after his money. Some would be after her calm, her peace. He had been, but he'd discovered it didn't exist; it wasn't peace, it was lack of awareness; it wasn't calm, it was indifference. She spoke to the horses the same way she spoke to him. She was absolutely fair, she showed no undue preference for either them or him. It was just that in the end she spent more time with them than him.

'Shall you tell the girls or shall I?'

'I think they know, James. Not about the divorce, but about us I mean.'

'I'll go down to Benenden myself in a couple of weeks.'

'I hear she's very beautiful.'

'Oh, who said that?'

'Several people actually. Tom Foster was the most enthusiastic of course.'

'He would be. What did he say?'

'Well you know what Tom is, James. Not exactly quotable.'

'I'd like to know, Laura. A kind of reference point.'

54

She looked across at him and he knew he was going to get hurt and he knew she would enjoy it. 'He said she is so pretty that he wouldn't know whether to frame her or screw her arse off – but he thought you wouldn't find it a problem.'

He'd always felt the cottage had low ceilings and he thought so now. The room seemed darker, gloomier, and he stood up in a hurry to go.

As the train wound its way back to London he thought about his life with Laura. There was so little he could remember. It was like a book, recently read, whose plot wasn't compelling enough to be recalled. All the same he had felt she was still part of his life as they had talked. Until the jibe from Tom Foster. It hadn't been accidental, it was deliberate, and despite the desultory conversation in the Mini he knew that he was on his own now. Well, himself and the girl. He wondered what her reaction would be. She'd asked about his wife and the girls right at the start, but it was to avoid complications, nothing to do with divorce or marriage. During his time with Laura, when he had frequently had vague thoughts of divorce and freedom, the fantasies had never included another marriage. Yet here he was, eager, perhaps desperate, for the girl to marry him, and almost afraid to ask her.

When he walked into the flat the girl was speaking on the telephone and when she turned and saw him she waved him over and said to the caller at the other end, 'Just a moment here he is, here's Dr. Hallet now – hang on.' She put her hand over the mouthpiece and said, 'Is somebody named Red Murphy – an American.'

He took the phone from her and said, 'Hi Red, where are you speaking from?' He listened. 'Well why not come right over. Doesn't matter, just take pot-luck or we'll go out to eat. O.K., we'll be waiting for you. About twenty minutes. Good.'

She said, 'Who is he? Sounds pretty lively.'

He sat down on the leather armchair and patted his lap. 'Come and sit on my lap. I've got something to tell you.'

He hadn't intended to tell her like this. In a hurry and without preparation, but some instinct made him want to tell her before anyone intruded on their lives. She seemed pleased that he had spoken about divorce to his wife and surprised that she'd agreed. Almost as if she didn't believe it.

'It's true Kris, and I want you to marry me.'

'How long before we could marry?'

'It's much easier these days. Probably no more than four to six weeks. So what do you say?'

She smiled. 'I say of course. You know I do.'

'You don't seem sure somehow.'

'Oh Jimmy, it's just very sudden, that's all. You've had time to think about it. I not.'

Then he was kissing her avidly and his hand was inside her sweater. The bell rang and reluctantly he released her and they both stood up. He walked rather unsurely to the door and opened it. The man with the beaming smile was well over six feet. A big plump ugly face with piggy eyes, and his smile showed uneven teeth. But the smile was the kind that really works, and it transformed the ugly face till it shone with a universal bonhomie that wouldn't be denied.

'Hi Red, come on in.'

'Jimmy boy, it's good to see ya.'

'Let me introduce Miss Kristina Olsen of Copenhagen. We're due to be married shortly.' He loathed himself for blurting it out like this but it was a kind of compulsion.

'You don't say. My, my – hello Kristina, well he sure is a lucky man. I guess there ain't no sisters at home like you.'

Then they were sitting round the low table drinking.

'What are you doing over here Red?'

'Oh I'm just doing a bit of research for a couple of senators.'

'How long you here for?'

'Six weeks, mebbe seven. All depends.'

'What's the research or is it classified?'

'Oh pretty routine stuff. We're looking for European research projects that are worthwhile but can't get off the ground, or stay off the ground, for lack of finance.'

'You'll be a popular man, Red, around these parts. There'll be plenty of takers.'

'Yeah, we know that but the Trust have a feeling that it doesn't want to be sold. We'd rather have things "drawn

56

to our attention" like the guys who write to *The Times.*
You know we must be boring Kristina silly.'

The girl shook her head. 'I'm not listening Red. I just
thinking woman thoughts about curtains and things. You
two keep talking.'

'We wanted your help Jimmy, or at least your advice.'

'I'm flattered.'

'No you're not. Will you help us – me?'

'You mean suggest deserving causes?'

'Yes.'

And for an hour he'd talked about men and teams
doing research that ranged from a cure for skin cancer
from seaweed to a new international monetary system that
would protect all individual currencies. Red Murphy had
made careful notes of names and addresses and telephone
numbers. They walked with Red, back to the Hilton and
they had dinner together at the hotel.

They took a taxi back to the flat and Hallet poured
himself a whisky and the girl a Coke, and as he pushed
it across to her he said, 'What did you think of Red?'

'Oh a nice man I think.'

'And what did you think of his mission over here?'

'Seems very generous, very American. And you will help
him?'

He shook his head and snorted into his whisky. 'He
doesn't need my help.'

'But he says for you to help him.'

'Sure, but he doesn't need my help to give money away.
There's a dozen men at the embassy in Grosvenor Square
who could give him the same advice. They could do it on
the phone.'

'Then why he say all this?'

'God knows Kris, but whatever Red Murphy wanted it's
not what he was talking about.'

CHAPTER VIII

When the detritus of the solid body of any cocktail party is examined it will fall into two elements. Those whom the hosts have pressed to stay behind when the others have gone, and those who have an inflated sense of their own importance. The second are the natural prey of ambassadors' wives who arrange the disappearance of waiters and sometimes the flickering of lights not far removed from shouting 'Time, gentlemen, please'. Madame Borowska, wife of His Excellency Stefan Borowski, was busy sorting the sheep from the goats. The Polish embassy in London was renowned for its entertainment and influence. It was the only Communist bloc embassy that had any pretensions to being European rather than Slav. And if it harboured an air of hussars and shakos there were few who would not count it a credit. The wine was the best and the girls were the prettiest. Its entertainment budget was lavish and less than half was paid by the KGB.

Hallet had been the guest of honour but had not been pressed to stay behind. His hostess felt that if she could dispose of him then all the others would surely follow.

'Ach, professor, do you like I fix for our car to take you – when you are ready of course?'

'Madame Borowska we were just waiting to say goodbye. We have our car outside.'

And so it was that at last the group of men could get together and review their evening's task. There was the Ambassador, two scientists and a senior man from the Polish secret police Z-11.

They talked for three hours and came to the conclusion that Hallet had not suspected their motives but that he was not working at any particular project at the moment and that his mind was over-occupied with the girl. Although a week or so later they changed their minds, that day they felt they had wasted their time.

*   *   *

Farrow had watched Hallet and the girl leave for the Polish embassy. An hour later it was really dark. His own man was in a parked Rover 2000 TC without lights, sitting on the back seat and almost impossible to see. The GRU men were not together. One was standing in a porch a few doors away from Hallet's flat and the other was in a Merc parked on the far side of Lower Belgrave Street where he could see the flat from good cover. He was bored and sure of himself. A bad combination.

He was smoking and watching the whole of his front. Farrow walked right round the block and at the bottom of Lower Belgrave Street he radioed to his man in the Rover. He was almost an arm's length from the Merc and he tapped with his nail on the radio. Off to the left in Ebury Street his man in the Rover leaned over and switched on his headlights. The man in the Merc threw down his cigarette stub and turned to look into Ebury Street. He went to turn his head as the cold of Farrow's pistol barrel touched the side of his face. But his reflexes were good and he froze even before Farrow said 'Hold it friend.' The man's hand was in the darkness of the car and he moved it gently across the seat beside him and then the pistol crashed against his face. It opened a long deep wound and the blood ran down warm to his neck and his collar felt wet and his right eye was closing fast. The Rover 2000 had swept round to face the Merc and Farrow's man opened the door of the Merc and pushed the bleeding man over. Farrow got in the back and they drove to the safe house in Pimlico. It wasn't a house but it was safe. It was the cover, the studio.

The man was too experienced to resist and he sat on the big wooden chair when Farrow waved him to it. The blood was still coming from the wound at the side of his face, but much slower, and from the big swollen eye ran a flow of tears. His good eye was quivering in an uncontrollable spasm. Farrow pulled up a chair and sat facing him.

'What's your name comrade?' And Farrow spoke in Russian and the man knew it was no use playing games.

'Stanislav Molak.'

'You a Pole?'

'Yes.'

'What were you doing?'

'Watching the Englishman Hallet.'

'Why?'

'Orders.'

'Who gives the orders?'

'The operation's controlled from the Polish embassy in Weymouth Street.'

'Who do you report to?'

'By telephone to extension 49.'

'How do you get paid?'

'An Irishman, I don't know his name. I think he works at Victoria Station. A clerk.'

'What are you looking for?'

'Just an 18-hour surveillance.'

'Is there a code word when you report?'

The man looked uneasy and then he nodded.

'Yes – it's Leningrad.'

'What shift do you do?'

'Two till ten.'

It was already ten-thirty so the embassy would already know about the intercept. Farrow went in the next room and made arrangements for a doctor to look at Molak's face and for him to be taken to the special section at Wormwood Scrubs.

He dialled the number of the Polish embassy and asked for extension 49. There was a silence and then a click and a rough voice said 'Yes, who is it?' in Russian. Farrow gave the password and there were a few moments' silence and then the man at the other end said a four letter word that takes seven letters in Russian, and slammed down the receiver.

Early next morning Farrow was reading through Anders's copy report. Security Signals reported unusual traffic on short-wave from the Polish embassy to Moscow and Warsaw. The code used was new and unbroken. There were no tails on Hallet since last night. Unidentified radio traffic was reported from the Croydon area. Transmissions were high-speed and would not respond to normal direction-finding equipment. A handwritten comment stated that the USA's National Security Agency had equipment in Fort George Meade that would pinpoint the transmitter if it could monitor at least four transmissions. Farrow phoned Anders to ask for this to be done. Anders was not sure that the Hallet operation had sufficient priority. Farrow reminded him of the report from the Chancellor of the Exchequer.

The Chancellor prided himself on his informal approach but faced with these particular men he took refuge in ritual. There was Sir John Walker, Director of Operations SIS; Ed Farrow SIS; Tad Anders SIS; Captain Sanders, Signals Security and Sir Martin Mace.

'Well, gentlemen, you all know why we are here. We are all concerned with the case of James Hallet. Colonel Farrow, I should like you to put us all in the picture. Right up to date.'

'Right sir. From Sir Martin we have strong indications that Hallet has information on some device or weapon of unusual destructive power. This information comes from Hallet himself. Ordinarily we don't take too much notice of this kind of stuff. Certainly not on so little information. But in this case there are several factors that make us concerned. In general, Hallet is a top scientist and he is not dependent on anyone for money. He's rich by any standards so he is not to be pressured by Government, industry or any kind of employment. Next, a GRU man was killed in Hallet's flat before he arrived but only shortly before. Then we have details of a surveillance team checking on Hallet. It's a GRU team not KGB and that's odd. I'll explain that in a moment. Another odd thing is that the GRU team is being operated out of the Polish embassy here not the Soviet embassy, which would be normal.

'Coming back to the involvement of the GRU. We would normally expect the KGB to be the interested party so far as Hallet or any other scientist is concerned. For the GRU to be involved it means that the Moscow Centre has decided that this is basically a military matter. There is abnormal signals traffic from the Poles to Moscow and Warsaw and they are using a really high-grade code which we haven't broken. We've asked through CIA for NSA assistance. They're the only people who could crack this inside six months. That's the main picture gentlemen.'

The Chancellor looked around the table but nobody seemed inclined to speak. Senior cabinet ministers were expected to do their own committee work with SIS. 'Tell me colonel, is there any kind of pressure that can be applied to Hallet – or persuasion for that matter?' he added with a quick but shifty look at Sir Martin.

'Mrs. Laura Hallet is applying for a divorce with custody of the two daughters. We picked this up in a routine check through all government departments. We had a guarded chat with Mrs. Hallet and I gather that it was being done at Hallet's request. Seems he's very keen to marry the girl he brought back from New York. I did wonder if we got her to drag her feet with the divorce whether we might do a deal of some sort. But it would only delay it for a time because he could go for a one-way application and I think he'd get it without the wife's agreement.'

'What about the girl?'

'What about her?'

'Is she a pressure point?'

'She's that all right but she's not likely to co-operate. She's an alien for one thing and she's getting the full treatment from Hallet. He's spending money like water. And I don't think she's an out-and-out hustler. I guess we could pick her up and use her as a hostage but we could come awfully unstuck awfully easily. I'd say count her as a last resort.'

'What about Sir Martin? Could he do anything more?' This was from Anders. And all eyes went to Sir Martin Mace who shrugged and leaned back in his chair. 'I don't think he'd tell me any more you know. If I say anything he may turn against me because he'll sense that I've told you people what I know.'

The Chancellor cut in, 'No Martin, I think you could be used to greater purpose.'

Farrow spoke again. 'I think we must bear in mind too that Hallet could give whatever he's got to the Soviets out of anger, if any pressure's put on him that can be attributed to us.'

Anders chipped in, 'Ed's quite right I'm sure sir, but I think his resources should be increased. I'd like to see him checking a bit more on the girl for instance.'

The Chancellor nodded. 'I agree. Well there seems to be nothing more I can contribute, we must leave it to the experts.'

CHAPTER IX

The girl stood with Hallet in the darkness and suddenly
the room was lighting up. Ceiling lights, wall lights on
paintings and angled lights on the big white desk. She
laughed, 'O.K. tell me how you make it. You not touch
anything.'

'They're thermal switches. They operated because our
body heat made them operate. They're convenient,
economical and a security precaution. If you look about
you'll see that there are no switches anywhere. If it's dark
enough and anyone is in here the lights go on.'

He took her hand and led her over to his desk and waved
her to a comfortable low chair at the side. There was a
row of buttons at the front of the desk and one had a
music note symbol and he said 'Look.' He struck a match
and held it near the button and in a second it lit up
and quadraphonic music poured into the room. Then the
music settled to a lower level. It was Strauss waltzes, then
he touched the button and it was half-way through the
storm in Beethoven's *Pastoral*. He touched it again and
there was Glen Miller, and again, and it was Joan Baez.
She smiled with amusement at the gadget and when he
asked her if she liked it, the music went lower in response
to his voice. Then he turned back to his desk.

'Honey, I shan't keep you more than a few minutes.'

He looked in his diary, made some calculations, went
over to the bookshelves and took down a book. More
writing, then he switched on the computer keyboard and
the visual display screen. Once again the screen filled
jerkily with numbers then when the last digit appeared he
touched a button and with a jump all the figures became
letters. Then when the screen was steady the letters went
out, one by one, from different parts of the screen, and
they read OMEGA MINUS. They held for a moment
then flicked off and the screen was blank.

The girl was touching her lips with an orange-red lipstick and as he turned and looked at her she grinned. 'Don't look like that. I think you go to spoil my lipstick.'

Farrow decided to put a little secondary pressure on the Pole in Wormwood Scrubs and he phoned Commander Bryant at Special Branch.

'I'd like you to put a bit of pressure on Molak. Interview him as if you've taken over his case. Be outraged and English and talk of a life sentence if he's lucky. I'd like to be able to see him this evening and it would help if his spirits were low.'

Hallet had given a small cocktail party for a few friends to meet his future bride and after the main body had departed he poured out drinks for the girl, Red Murphy and Sir Martin Mace. When they were settled Hallet had looked across at Sir Martin and said,

'Martin, Red here is looking for deserving scientific causes to support. Got any ideas?'

'What sort of return are you looking for Red?'

'No returns at all Martin. It's Trust funds.'

'Ah yes, lovely thought. Despite his present attitude there was a time when our James was very glad of Trust funds.'

'That so James?'

'I suppose so but the important thing is how they're administered. Martin was good at it. It wasn't his dough and he was generous with it.'

'And out of that you invented "Plasticond"?'

'Oh, invent is a big, big word. "Plasticond" was a piece of thinking. The Trust gave me time to think.'

'And now you don't need a Trust, you've got all the bread and all the time.' Mace watched Hallet's face as he sought to answer the question.

'In a way, Red. The trouble now is lack of purpose, lack of drive.'

'What kind of work do you do now anyway?'

Hallet turned and looked at Murphy. 'Sometimes I wonder, Red, sometimes I wonder. In the last year I've had one piece of chain reaction thinking, and only one, and it would have been better unthought.' He leaned forward

65

almost eagerly. 'You know it's so odd. We can't – none of us can – think good thoughts just because we want to. I cannot control my thinking in any way. I can pull out facts from my subconscious as if it were some sort of data bank but when you *really* think, when you invent that is, you have a thought that isn't in your data bank. You make a thought that is absolutely new, no source, no reason, no anything. It's like Joan of Arc's voices. It's as new to you as the people you tell it to.' He laughed. 'I'm sorry, I'm being a bore.'

Nobody spoke and the spell was broken and lifts were offered and taxis called.

Venturi had called off the full-scale surveillance of Hallet as soon as his man had been picked up. He had reported the news to Moscow and had received immediate instructions to lie low until further orders came through.

Farrow looked across the rough table at Molak. There was a big dressing on the right-hand side of his face and the bandage that held it went across his right eye.

'How is the face, Molak?'

The man shrugged and said nothing.

'Have you heard when you come up for trial?'

Molak's one blue eye looked at Farrow and he said, 'There won't be any trial comrade. You know that as well as I do. We shall all do whatever your master decides.' Farrow immediately noticed that Molak had used the Georgian word *batano* for master instead of the Russian word.

'Which part of Georgia do you come from comrade?'

The half seen face was twisted in a smile. 'From Tbilisi, but it's a long time ago.' Farrow pulled out a pack of cigarettes and pushed them with a lighter across the table. The nicotined fingers reached for them eagerly. When the man had lit the cigarette, Farrow said 'Where did you do your training?'

'At the Centre.'

'Dzerzhinski Street or Kuznetský Most?'

'Both, at different times.'

'Is Abakumov still in charge of training?'

'You're well-informed, comrade. Yes, he's still in charge.'

'Let's see, when was his father executed – 1956 was it?'

'1954, they did Likhachev at the same time.'

'Ah yes, Deputy boss of Special Cases.'

They were both fencing and probing but Farrow decided to take the plunge.

'Do we do a deal Molak?'

'Depends on the deal.'

'Let's say you get your freedom and a small pension.'

'Sounds sensible to me. What do you want to know?'

'Who's in charge of the operation. Where is he and what's it all about?'

Molak looked at him cautiously with his one eye. 'How about we do it piece for piece? I give you his name and you let me out. Then I tell you the rest against my pension.'

'How about we compromise on the name and the location? I'll trade the pension for the operation later.'

'How much later?'

'Tomorrow.' Farrow's eyebrows were raised in query and Molak looked away and said, 'I don't know all you want to know anyway.'

Farrow nodded, 'O.K. Molak, start talking and we'll see how we go.'

'The set up is apparat two. The boss-man is named Venturi and . . .'

Farrow interrupted. 'You mean Sergei Venturi?'

'Yes – you know of him?'

'But he's not KGB he's GRU.'

'Sure, but the GRU have been given the apparat for this operation.'

'O.K. carry on.'

'He's in this country, somewhere to the south of London. That's all I know about him.'

'What about the operation?'

'It's something to do with this fellow Hallet. We've got to watch all his contacts so they can be checked on.' He put both his hands on the table. 'I assure you that's all I know. It's a very slow operation and all I do is surveillance.'

'What about the contacts? Any excitements there?'

67

'Only one – a man they checked on and are still watching.'

'Who is he?'

Molak looked embarrassed. 'I'll trade that for the pension.'

'That could take me a day to fix.'

'I can wait.'

It took Farrow ten hours and he'd only fixed a lump sum payment of £2,000. The official car waited for the prison gates to open, and then he stepped out in the quadrangle and walked across to the Governor's office. He had guessed that Molak would feel encouraged if he was taken from the cell and brought to less formal surroundings.

Molak stood up when Farrow came in. The bandage had gone and had been replaced by a large plaster.

'Sit down Molak.'

When they were both seated Farrow started. 'I'm afraid I can't arrange a pension. I can offer a lump sum payment of £2,000 – that's all.'

'In German marks?'

'Sure.'

'O.K.'

'Tell me about the man and the operation.'

Ten minutes later Farrow had made the necessary arrangements for Molak and was on his way back to the boat. He reckoned he'd certainly had his £2,000 worth.

CHAPTER X

A phone call from Hallet's solicitors had vaguely hinted at deliberate delays by Laura, and he had snapped back that they should contact her at once and make clear that he would himself apply for a divorce if there was any further delay. The episode had left him tense and on edge and he recognized that his various problems were no nearer solution. He also realized that he was tired without having worked, and for him that was a sign of near break-down. It had happened once before and he didn't want it again, especially right now.

He called to the girl who was in the bathroom.

'Kristina, shall we go away for a few days?'

'Come in and speak nearer.'

He walked in and sat in the cane armchair. She was lying in the bath with lather up to her chin.

'What you say about going away?'

'Shall we go to the country for a few days?'

'That would be nice. Where we go?'

'I've got a house down in Kent. We could go there.'

'Yes, that sounds good, shall we buy food?'

'No, we can buy food in the village.'

Farrow lit the Calor gas fire and put it up on the working surface of the galley so that its heat spread over the whole of the saloon. Then he pulled across the red phone and called Anders.

'Tad, I'm going over to scrambler.'

'O.K.'

'Right now. A couple of real bombs this afternoon Tad. Do you have a file on Venturi? Last I heard of him he was a major in the GRU.'

'Yes, we have a fair old stack on Venturi. He's a colonel now by the way. What about him?'

'He's here Tad. He's running this Hallet operation for the GRU, using a KGB apparat.'

69

'That upgrades this quite a few notches Ed. Any idea where he is?'

'All that Molak could say is that he's not far from London and it's south of London. Not very helpful.'

'Better than nothing. It fits quite well because Venturi is the GRU's electronics king. He knows his stuff all right. Now I'll get a check on up-to-date stuff on this fellow and maybe we can meet tomorrow morning early.'

'O.K. by me, I'd like a back check done that he's not in Moscow and any details of when and how he left.'

'Sure, I'll do that Ed. What's the second bomb-shell?'

'The Russians have been keeping a complete check on all Hallet's contacts since a few days after he got back. There's just one interesting guy by the name of Murphy – Benjamin Murphy, and he's registered at the Hilton. I've checked. He's met Hallet on five known occasions.'

'Jesus Christ Ed, that's Red Murphy and he's CIA.'

'That's just what my little man said.'

'He's an old friend of Hallet's so maybe it's a coincidence.'

'Not for me it isn't, not for me.'

'I think you're right. He'd have contacted us if it was straight. My God, what a bloody circus.'

'That means we've got the GRU, the CIA, and us, all sniffing round Hallet.'

'You'd better contact Sir John and have a review. I'll contact you tomorrow morning early.'

Venturi went into the darkroom and switched on the transceiver. Then he went back to the main room and switched on the colour TV and tuned in to 'Match of the Day'. His radio contact with Moscow was in an hour and it helped if the set was warmed up well in advance. Leeds were playing Newcastle. Leeds always seemed to be playing someone on Saturday nights.

He tuned in to Moscow on 173 kHz and he was ready with paper and pencil waiting for the closing announcement. Then it came, and listeners were invited to send their queries to Radio Moskva, paztnitskaja ulitza 25, Moskva, and then they gave the telephone number 'Moskva 2336356'. And finally they gave another address 'ulitza Malaja Sadovaja 2, Leningrad'. Venturi spent ten minutes

70

with a piece of graph paper and then he was ready.

He tuned to the coded wavelength and put on the headphones. He hated this bit. For basic security he couldn't have the transmission coming through a speaker, but with the headphones on he couldn't hear anything in the room or the house, and that made him feel insecure. Then the carrier wave came on and he turned the slow-gear-tuner very slowly until the carrier-wave level-meter showed eight, and then he waited. Then the Morse came and he was getting it down on his signal pad. There were nearly seven minutes of transmission and then there was just the hiss of the carrier wave and then empty silence like a hole in the air.

It took more than an hour to decode the message from Moscow. It instructed him to contact Hallet and to use the codeword Omega Minus and watch his reaction and pursue the subject if possible. Moscow had reliable information that this codeword was known, and may have been designed by Hallet to cover his latest work.

The white Lamborghini slid eastwards out of Tunbridge Wells and then took the minor road to Frant. A few miles farther on it turned due north and at the next crossroads they waited for a tractor to pass. Then it was due east and he felt a sudden pleasure as the road turned at the hop gardens and swept over the bridge and up the hill to Goudhurst. At the pond they turned left past 'The Vine' and eased their way down the twisting lanes to a square white cottage that stood back from the road.

Hallet got out and opened the white wooden gates and drove into the drive and alongside the house. A small white wooden sign said 'Lidwell's Lodge'. The house itself was a typically Kentish building. Square, in white clapboard with carefully raked roofs in Kentish tiles. The garden gave on to an orchard and in the late afternoon light the apples looked pale and luminous. The garden sloped quickly and gave a panoramic view of a green-clad valley whose detail was lost in the evening mist. Above the mist they could see a church tower on the other side of the valley and as the late sun lit the warm stone it stood out like a ship at night on the ocean of wet mist.

Half an hour later their luggage was in, and a log fire was spurting and crackling in the stone hearth. It was a cosy house. The girl was sitting with her legs drawn up beneath her and there was an opened bottle of wine and some sandwiches. Hallet had his feet up on a leather footstool as he talked and drank. The light from the fire was the only light in the room and it cast its light upwards, and their faces looked strange and mysterious.

'Tomorrow I'll take you to see the cathedral at Canterbury. You'll like that.'

'How long we stay here?'

'Oh, see how it goes. A week – ten days maybe.'

'It make you feel more relaxed down here, yes?'

'Yes, I suppose it does Kris. I just wish the divorce was over and we could be married tomorrow.'

'Is that all you worry about? What about the girls?'

'They won't worry. I'll see them almost as much as I do now. Benenden – their school – is near here. I must go over and see them during the week.'

'So no other things to worry?'

'There's something to do with my work that worries me.'

'How it worry you? Tell me.'

'I don't know what to do about it.'

'O.K. why not you forget it then? Do nothing.'

'That could be dangerous. I found something that has no use at all except to destroy things. And it does that so easily I don't like to think about it.' He looked across at her and was silent. A log sparked and settled in the hearth. He looked back at her. 'You only need one and that could blackmail the world. All the developed world anyway.'

'Does such a thing cost much, much money to make?'

He looked up at the beams in the shadows of the ceiling. 'Not quite £20.'

Anders parked his Jag in Royal Hospital Road and walked down to the Embankment. Although it was barely six o'clock there were lights on in *My Joanna* and it was too misty to see anything on the other side of the river, except the trees in Battersea Park.

There were two steaming cups of coffee on the saloon table and he sat down and put his case on the seat beside him.

'I've got photostats of everything on Venturi for you and I'll leave those.' He pulled out a notebook. 'I had a message via Warsaw during the night. Venturi left Leningrad exactly three weeks ago yesterday. Left from the small military air-field at Moscow with a landing at Berlin an hour later. Left there in a civil aircraft – a Cessna with French mark-ings, believed heading for a holiday in northern France. Nothing else.'

'Anything on Murphy?'

'Yes. A friend of Hallet for at least ten years. His cover has generally been as an assistant to senate committees and individual senators. It's thought that most of them didn't know he was CIA. Looks like Hallet certainly doesn't know. He did a roving commission reporting on security at the US embassies in Moscow, Prague, Warsaw, Budapest and Vienna. I guess the Russians are more aware of him than we are. Has a good educational background including MIT and six months at NASA. Well liked by everybody. There's a detailed background piece in the file here.'

'Any views as to what he's doing over here?'

'Not as yet. My impression is that he's used on high-grade missions of short duration. You can do a tail job on him and check if he's making other continuous contacts apart from Hallet.'

'It looks as if everybody's come to the conclusion that Hallet is on to something and now we've got the CIA, the GRU and us sitting around trying to find out what it's all about.'

'And when somebody's found it out. Then what?'

'Depends what it is.'

'Keep in touch and I'll pass anything I get as soon as I get it.'

Venturi checked again on the ordnance survey sheet. He'd been given a map reference in a message from Moscow and urgent instructions to provide some piece, however small, of the crashed FE-111E. He had flown to Newcastle and then hired a Capri and headed north.

The landscape at the approaches to Rothbury is stark and wild. Heather and couch grass and sharp outcrops of granite and basalt. It was high above sea level and no trees grew. In the distance were the acres of sitka spruce planted by the Forestry Commission: pathetic, monotonous, unimaginative forestry, it somehow suited the moon-crater landscape.

There were low, dry walls snaking over the contours. Protecting what from what? In many directions the grass and heather had burnt in the summer sun. Venturi took a bearing on a distant peak and another on a col only half a mile away. He pencilled the bearings. on the map and saw that he had a mile farther to go. He turned back to look at the car but it was already in dead ground and out of sight.

Twenty minutes later he had arrived and the map reference was accurate because he could see the scars of the impact of fuselage and engines. The earth was still raw and exposed. There was a flattish outcrop of rock and he put down his haversack and the map, and sat down for a moment as he scanned the area for debris. There had not been a series of impacts. Just one, and a slide of about 400 feet. There would be debris distributed up to at least a half-mile radius and he marked up a piece of graph paper and set down the ordnance map co-ordinates. To the west was a steep hill with outcrops of rock, but on all the other sides was purple heather, coarse grass and slabs of rock that were thrusting through the thin top soil like ugly fangs. It was going to be a long job and he marked off the first square on the graph paper and took out a small plastic bag from a packet. Nearly seven hours later he had a dozen small bags numbered with references to the squares where their contents had been picked up. There was a wide variety of debris ranging from metal and plastic, to wires and bits and pieces of instruments. There were some pieces that were quite large and heavy and it had taken him three journeys to the car before they were all packed carefully in the boot.

Venturi stayed the night in Alnwick and he was tempted to drive out and look at the perimeter of RAF Boulmer. But his trained caution analysed it as a risk without a prize. He already knew exactly what it looked like from photographs and sketches.

He felt strangely at home in the wild Northumbrian landscape. The bare hills, and the slopes covered with evergreen spruce were typical of acres of countryside around Leningrad and Moscow, but the Russians had too much land to need to grind a meal for flying flocks of sheep from a soil without sub-soil that grew only this coarse, acid grass. Alnwick itself was like a miniature Kiev. Stone battlements that were for fighting and repelling, and not for decoration; a small walled town sitting on a trade route.

He looked over the debris without disturbing it but there were no clues for him. It would need a forensic laboratory. The plastic bags were in the Polish diplomatic bag the next day and in Moscow the following morning.

CHAPTER XI

The Trident had banked just before Malmö and had had
to come round tightly across Saltholm Island. It had left
Copenhagen to the north and made a clean landing at
Kastrup. Farrow had only an overnight bag and he'd
walked across to the taxis and with routine caution had
waited for two girls to come up and take the first one
and then he had signalled to the second. 'Hafnia Hotel,
Vester Voldgade.'

After he had checked into the hotel and his bag had been
taken to his room, he phoned a local number. Fifteen
minutes later he was in the restaurant and when he'd
ordered he sat back and looked around. Everywhere was
teak and glass and it reminded him of the boat. He felt at
home.

There was a pianist who was playing 'As time goes by',
and Farrow was so absorbed by the lush lazy chords, that
for a moment he didn't notice the man who stood at the
table. He was wearing an anorak and pale blue denim
trousers. And he was blond and brown-faced and he held
out his hand. 'Anderson, Mr. Farrow. Shall I sit down?'
And they sat, and talked, and planned.

Knud Anderson was single and twenty-eight, stocky and
solid, and he taught 'The principles of animal feeding' at
the university. He wasn't the SIS man in Copenhagen, but
he was used and paid by the SIS on a variety of jobs
where they were concerned to leave no connection to their
man, and to protect his cover as one of Scandinavia's lead-
ing sellers of Rolls-Royces and Jaguars.

It was the initial check on the address that Kristina Olsen
had given that had made them steer clear of the SIS man.
The home address was in Ny Vestergade, opposite the
National Museum and was a typical upper-class apartment. The business premises were alongside the harbour
and the products were high-grade amplifiers for hi-fi sys-

76

tems. There was a small brass plate outside the town apartment and it carried the simple legend 'Arne og Olga Olsen'.

They hadn't liked the Olga bit and a check at the police department had confirmed that Mrs. Olsen had come to Denmark just after the war. Her maiden name was Olga Spenskaya and she'd been a member of a Russian trade mission. She had been an unimportant member and her defection had not made the headlines as it was clearly because she wanted to marry Olsen. The Russians had kicked up a stink for a couple of weeks but it had eventually all died down.

Olsen's record was unremarkable. University combined with some radio work for the Danish underground. Then when the war was ended and he'd got his degree, a stint in one of the bigger electronics outfits on the management side. He'd been in business on his own for nearly ten years and was considered to be doing well. He did a large amount of export, lived well, and both he and his equipment were well thought of in London and New York.

Despite all this the Russian wife rang bells for SIS and they spent time checking the background. There was nothing much in their results but they remained cautious.

Farrow and Anderson arranged to meet later that evening. The district around Nikolaj Kirke is known to the locals as 'the minefield' and the name comes not from any war but from the nature of its habitués. It's the home of all those small music and dance spots where three beers gets you a seat for the evening and where the clients are sailors, artists and their models, and, at the beginning of the term, students.

As Farrow walked down the narrow streets the late sun lit the yellow painted buildings and cast black shadows from the projecting hoists that had been used a hundred years ago to lift and stow the cargoes from the canals. There was an iodine smell from the sea and a sharp breeze rattled the shutters. The 'Ny Kakadu' was crowded and when Farrow went down the steps it was difficult to recognize anyone in the dim smoke-laden light. Then there was a wave and a shout and he could see Anderson waving to him from a table in an alcove. He was introduced to a small man with a pale face and sparse hair. 'Chief, this is Paul,

77

and I've done a deal with him. Just up to you now to give the go-ahead.'

Despite a lock-picking course with the Portsmouth police, the complex locks on Copenhagen town houses were not within Farrow's scope. Paul was considered to be the local expert and Farrow and Anderson were going to rely on his expertise. He'd had a passing look at the lock on the Olsens' apartment and he estimated that he would need fifteen seconds to have it open without damage. He was being paid in advance and would just leave the door ajar and walk on.

The Olsens had left town in the late afternoon and it had been checked that they were motoring to Elsinore for the last of the season's *Hamlets* by an English Shakespeare group. It was estimated that they would not be back before midnight at the earliest.

At nine o'clock Farrow and Anderson stood talking in Ny Westergade. There were lights in the museum and a few cars, but no pedestrians in the street apart from themselves. Paul walked past them on the other side of the road and they watched him ring the bell and wait. He'd rung the bell again but this time he turned and looked up and down the road and then walked off slowly towards the canal. When they walked over, the door was open, and they waited for a moment and then walked in.

Steep stairs led up to the hallway of the apartment. There was a large room arranged as a combined living- and dining-room. They checked the three bedrooms first but these were simply furnished and the drawers and shelves contained little more than clothes and simple jewellery. They came back to the big room. The ceiling sloped down to crown the tops of the windows and on the long wall was a large stove with blue and white ceramic tiles and beautiful, polished copper doors. Even though it was barely autumn the stove was already lit and the whole room smelled of warm wood. There were rows of books on wooden shelves. They seemed to be either just reference books or novels. The big writing desk in the corner was not locked and appeared to be the only place used for keeping papers of any kind. Farrow and Anderson went through every drawer and there was nothing of interest.

78

Just letters, bills for household goods and oddments of writing materials. When it was obvious that Farrow had come to the end of his fruitless search Anderson spoke. 'Sometimes these old desks have a secret drawer Mr. Farrow. Would you like me to try and find it?'

The secret drawer was a thin box-like shape in the back panelling and the contents were held together by an elastic band. There were two passports, one each for the Olsens, birth certificates for the Olsens, for a daughter Kristina, and a boy who had been born in 1950. A death certificate for the boy which showed that he had died aged two of an unidentified virus infection. There was a formal letter of thanks for war service in the Danish Resistance from King Frederik IX and a slightly more effusive letter of thanks for services rendered, from the United States Office of Strategic Services, signed with a flourish by 'Wild' Bill Donovan himself.

In a square case was a white and red enamelled medal with a cross and crowns and a silk ribbon in white with fine red selvedges. Anderson looked impressed and identified it as the Order of Dannebrog, and it seemed that they weren't handed out with the 'smørrebrød'. There were a few school reports showing that Kristina was doing average well. A degree on parchment for electrical engineering from Copenhagen University. There was a marriage certificate and papers covering the incorporation of Olsen's company. There were share certificates covering a variety of investments including a substantial holding in blue chips. Apart from his own company the major holding was in IBM.

They carefully checked the rest of the room and then checked the whole apartment a second time. There was nothing more.

Farrow made a few more routine inquiries but there was no significant information. He checked on the newspaper files for the story of when the wife had defected, but it hadn't even been a nine days' wonder. It was out of the news by the fifth day.

Ed Farrow was back on his boat at Cadogan Pier the following morning. It seemed there was no reason to suspect a Russian link just because of the Olsen woman.

79

CHAPTER XII

It took Venturi almost four hours to check where Hallet and the girl had gone, but the garage in Lower Belgrave Street where Hallet kept the Lamborghini provided the final clue. The cottage in Goudhurst had not been in the GRU dossier on Hallet. It wasn't in the SIS dossier either.

Venturi studied the appropriate maps at the house in Sanderstead and then booked himself a room by telephone at 'The Vine' in Goudhurst. It was almost closing time when he turned the MG into the forecourt.

The next day was a Sunday and Venturi spent the whole of the afternoon reconnoitring Lidwell's Lodge and the valley behind the cottage. He found a pathway overgrown with ferns, and a hedge with a foam of convolvulus that led off from the Marden road which gave him cover to the edge of an apple orchard that bordered the sloping lawns of the cottage. There was a cedarwood garden shed half-covered by a wild and straggling blackberry in the garden itself and it looked as if it would be a safe observation post at night.

When Venturi walked down the lane that evening it had been dark for over an hour but he had seen the pale shape of the Lamborghini parked in the drive. It was almost eight-thirty when he turned down the path from the Marden road.

When he came to the edge of the orchard he stood and looked up towards the house, but the ground was too steep and the cottage was in dead ground. He turned and looked back across the valley and as he did there was a flash of summer lightning that lit the rows of apple trees and washed across the hills on the far side of the valley. There was no thunder, but with the second flash a breeze rustled the leaves and the apple-loaded branches swung and creaked.

It was almost twenty minutes later when he got to the wooden shed. There were lights on inside the white cottage, and as he stood in the shadows Venturi could see both

Hallet and the girl. They were eating at a long pinewood table and there was a man with his back to the window. Venturi watched them eating and talking and the two men looked serious and intent on their conversation. Finally they stood up and he saw that the second man was Mace, the man who appeared in Hallet's dossier as his financial adviser and confidant. The two men settled in armchairs and Hallet poured some kind of wine for both of them.

The girl had left the room and some instinct told Venturi that the key to the operation was being cut as he watched. The flash of vivid lightning crackled and the thunder came immediately, shaking the ground as the wind gusted and tore at the trees. The earth smelt wet even before the rain came hissing down.

Venturi moved by reflex and hurried through the orchard and down the wet, muddy, pathway to the Marden road. When he got to the gate of the cottage his clothes were sodden and the rain still came down heavy and fast so that the road was a moving stream. It was Hallet who opened the white door.

They had picked up Sir Martin at Tunbridge station. The girl sensed that Hallet was on edge and she had been glad when he had phoned Sir Martin with the invitation to dinner. It had been one of those hot and sunny days the English autumn sometimes offers to its devotees, and they had sat in the lengthening shadows of the garden until she had called them to eat. She had halved some Jaffa oranges, filled them with sorbet and chilled them till they were frosted. It was when she had served these that Hallet had spoken.

'Martin, this thing I told you about, have you thought any more about it?'

Mace had a silver spoon half-way to his mouth. He lowered it slowly to his plate, touched his mouth with his napkin and looked across at Hallet.

'James, I had an idea when you phoned me that it might be this thing that was worrying you. Of course I've thought about it, but I have too little to go on.

'You've told me that it's a devastating weapon. I assume

it caused the death of the chap with the radio, the naval rating and maybe it even caused the American plane to crash. That is all I know.

'What worries me most is you saying that others may have started putting two and two together and guessing what it's all about. That could leave you in great danger.

The girl leaned across the table and put her hand on Hallet's arm. 'Let me leave you and Martin to talk.'

Hallet shook his head impatiently and turned to Sir Martin as if he hadn't heard. 'No, I don't think they have started guessing yet – there's not enough for them to go on, but when they do the clues are there – not about what it is exactly, but enough to identify the general area and that will certainly point them at me.

'I was at a conference in San Francisco some months back and I touched on the necessity to explore what I referred to as "the minus factors". We've spent a lot of time on the plus factors – reduce the surface tension of water and you make it wetter, so we end up with detergents. But we need to go on automatically from there and explore how to make water less wet or how to make dry drier.

'We don't do this because scientists cost money and unless we can see some sort of pay-off we don't let them start. Pure research these days is getting less and less and it's almost entirely medical. I went on about this and if people start looking into those things like the plane crash and the *Pillager* they may look for a link, and as I was in the area at the time testing an improved Ministry device they'd surely link it to me.

Hallet was leaning forward and Mace could feel his urgency and tension. He had finished the sorbet and was absent-mindedly tapping the frozen orange peel. Without looking directly at Hallet he said, 'Jimmy, I must tell you that people have already started putting the pieces together. I don't think they know very much but they've certainly started the machinery.'

'Is this our lot or somebody else?'

'Our lot and certainly the Soviets.'

'The man killed in the flat?'

'Yes.'

'They told me it was a mistake – a political thing.'

'I suppose it was in a way. It was a Pole working for the Russians who was killed.'

'What shall I do, Martin, it's driving me mad?'

'What do you want to do?'

'I suppose I just want to put the clock back. Wipe it all out – make it like I never thought of it.'

'Why not just pass it over to our chaps?'

'Martin I loathe them – both lots – what have they done to us. The Tories can't make us into successful capitalists and Labour can't run a socialist economy; we've always had the worst of both worlds. It isn't that they've tried the bold experiment and failed, they haven't tried anything, ever. They couldn't resist using this like a blunt instrument.'

'And the Russians?'

'Oh forget 'em. The greatest resources in the world in minds and material and what do they do – create a cross between Swansea on Sunday night and Dachau, and spread it over a third of the world.'

'So?'

'Have you spoken to Laura?'

'About the divorce you mean?'

Hallet nodded, and Mace knew then that Hallet was a sick man. His mind a jumble of tensions and worries. The good brain was turning madly and desperately, like a rat on a laboratory wheel. Hallet needed help and Mace guessed that he was ready to accept it.

'James, I've not been idle on your problem but you did restrict what I could do. I've probably gone beyond your brief but I think it's time you talked to someone who can really help you. Someone who could give you the advice you need. So how about your letting me arrange it?'

To his surprise Hallet nodded, 'You're right Martin, it's already gone on too long. Who've you got in mind?'

'I had in mind Dickie Thorne. He's a good friend of mine and you're going to need someone at Cabinet level in the end.'

Hallet looked drawn and near breaking-point and Mace wished he could get Thorne down tonight; Hallet was near the end of his tether. The dynamism that had been there while he talked of his feelings was gone. But he was nodding his head and he said very quietly, 'Yes please Martin, I'd better do that before there's more trouble. When shall we meet and where?'

'I'll ask him to come down here – I'm sure he will.' The bell rang at the front door. Hallet stood up slowly and said 'I'll see who it is.'

When he opened the door he saw the man in the soaking wet clothes.

'Good heavens you are in a state, what can I do for you?'

The stranger whose car had broken down had been invited in and had used the telephone. A car would be coming for him from London. Meanwhile his clothes were drying and he sat in one of Hallet's old dressing-gowns drinking a whisky. Sir Martin Mace had left for the station in the village taxi and the girl had retired to bed.

Hallet sat with the caller and they had listened to the hi-fi and talked of Dublin and a mutual friend in the Dublin hierarchy. It was when he noticed his visitor tapping his bare foot to Fats Waller playing 'My very good friend the milkman' that he ventured to say, 'Forgive my rudeness but I'm guessing from your accent that you're an American, but I can't do better than that. Is it New York?'

The man in the dressing-gown turned his head and looked across at Hallet. He didn't speak for several moments and then he said quite quietly, 'No, Dr. Hallet, I'm not an American but I have lived in the States. I'm from Moscow and I came to this country to make contact with you.'

Hallet looked bewildered. 'You know my name – but what's this all about? What are you doing here? What's all this about Moscow? Why do you want to contact me?'

'What I say will probably sound stupid but it's the truth. Some of my colleagues are very worried. They think you have made some sort of discovery that might threaten our country's security. I would like to ask if this is true. And if it is true I would like to ask what we can do to persuade you not to let it be used against us. I am authorized to negotiate any deal that might interest you.'

'What gave your colleagues this idea?'

'We learned from a routine report that you had been temporarily attached to the RAF station at Boulmer. From other sources we learned about an explosion on a Navy tug and an American fighter plane crash. Both these things happened on the same night at the same time, in the same area near Boulmer, and at that time you yourself were there. We understood that some new weapon was being tested and that you were conducting the tests.'

'Is that all?'

Venturi smiled and gave a Gallic shrug, 'That's quite a lot Doctor, but no, it's not all we know. I'm quite prepared to be frank. We are quite, quite sure that there is something, and that you are responsible, we do not know very much more. That is why I am here.'

Hallet leaned back in his armchair and his eyes looked suddenly alert, as if the confrontation had brought him some sort of relief. 'And what do you expect me to do Mister ... I didn't get your name.'

'I'm Sergei Venturi and I am an officer in the Soviet intelligence services.'

'Do the British authorities know you are in this country?'

'I should think they know by now.'

'Aren't you likely to be arrested?'

'Oh really Doctor Hallet, I am a diplomat and I am not committing an offence in talking to you.'

'And you think I might have discovered some new weapon and that I might sell you the details?'

'Not at all. I'm sure you've already got all the money you need. Apart from that we don't see you as an enemy. You gave us the formulation for your plastic conductor and you could easily have made us pay. We are already in your debt. It's your help we ask. Your co-operation.'

Hallet looked at Venturi. This man was no fool, those pale blue eyes he'd seen before, they reminded him of the acrid smell in the Lion House at the zoo, and a puma that paced up and down, its body coiled with muscle and its flat head turning in quick anger as the blue eyes caught a movement in the crowd. And just as with the puma, the man had a live and vital attraction. It would be useless and dangerous to send this man packing. Even if he went, which was doubtful, he'd be back.

85

'I'll think about what you have said. Phone me here tomorrow afternoon. You probably know the number already.'

'I'll phone you in the afternoon.'

'Where can I contact you?'

'The Soviet embassy would do. I take it that you will not be mentioning our talk to anyone else?'

'Nobody official.'

Venturi looked as if he were going to protest and then shrugged and said nothing. Half an hour later he had left the cottage in his dry clothes and with an upward glance at the watery moon and the low clouds, he had walked up the lane. As he moved away he turned and waved as if he were an old friend.

At the telephone kiosk near the pond Venturi made a call to London. He then walked slowly back to about thirty yards from the cottage, and waited. There were no lights on now and the whole valley was still. He heard the shrill exasperated bark of a vixen with cubs, and sheep sent stones rolling as they stumbled in the field behind him.

Hallet hadn't denied that he had something, but it was going to need a lot of talk before he had any real news for Moscow. Maybe they'd have to send over one of the scientists to soften him up. This could be the pay-off for Lementov, they'd let him play the protesting dissident for over a year. The anti-party nomination for the Nobel peace prize, the interviews with western journalists and the usual slim volume of turgid verse smuggled out and published in the west. Venturi had thought it a waste of time but right now it could be useful. Then he heard the faint sound of a car engine and a few minutes later a torch glowed for a moment and he went to meet them. Twenty minutes later three men were in position with strict orders covering what to do in most circumstances. Venturi was asleep in the back of the car being driven back to London.

CHAPTER XIII

The boat was riding uneasily against a flooding tide and the nylon warps were snapping from slack to strain as solid blocks of brown Thames water thrust and rolled against the hull. But Farrow was deep asleep when the phone rang. He pulled on the trailing wire to bring the instrument alongside his bunk.

'Farrow.'

'Rogers here, sir. I'm calling from Goudhurst.'

'Where's that?'

'In Kent sir, just east of Tunbridge Wells.'

'What's going on down there?'

'I was watching Sir Martin and he came down here. Was picked up at the station by Hallet and brought back to a cottage in the village here. It appears to be owned by Hallet and he's staying here with the girl – Miss Olsen that is.'

'Go on.'

'Sir Martin left some time ago. Looked like a taxi taking him back to the station. I decided to stay on sir. I've reported to Central Security and they're taking over Sir Martin while I hang on down here.'

'Why's that Rogers?'

'Well, just before Sir Martin left a man came running into the lane and then he knocked at the cottage door and they let him in. There'd been a violent storm and he was soaking wet. He stayed on for a good time after Sir Martin had gone. The storm was well over when he left and he went up to the phone in the village, made a longish call and then he went back to the lane and hung round for nearly two hours till a car came. There were three men apart from the driver and he talked to them and they've staked out the cottage and they're still there.'

'You get the number of the car?'

'Yes sir, it's one from the Polish embassy. No CD plates and it took the chap back towards the main London road.

87

There's an "all-cars" out for observation only. Central Security gave me your number and told me to report to you.'

'Anything else?'

'Yes sir, I think the man who was here was Venturi. I've only seen routine photographs but I'd say it was him.'

Farrow gave new orders to Rogers and then called Anders at Central Security. Sir Martin Mace was a little testy when he was phoned but agreed to a meeting as soon as he had spoken to the Chancellor.

Richard Thorne was listening to what Mace had to say and sat comfortably in his chair looking at the ceiling. When Mace had finished Thorne reached for the phone and told his secretary to hold calls and cancel his next two appointments. Then he turned to Mace.

'Did a man call at the cottage while you were there?'

Mace looked surprised. 'Yes, a man who'd been caught in the storm. The poor devil was soaked. How on earth did you know?'

'The poor devil was in fact a Soviet agent – and a very senior one too.'

'Good God – does Hallet know, has anyone warned him?'

Thorne looked across at Mace and wondered why such shrewd men could be such fools when it wasn't a question of money.

'You're assuming he needs warning Martin. Our man tells us that when your visitor left the cottage he waved in quite a friendly manner. Have you spoken to Hallet this morning, and asked him about the man?'

'No, I haven't spoken to him at all.'

'I've got the feeling Martin, that up to now you have not taken the Soviet interest very seriously. Thought we were exaggerating maybe.

'I'd like you to call Hallet. Just a friendly word to say you're going to see me in the next hour or so, and has he had any other thoughts.'

In case there was any doubt that this was an order Thorne shoved across a red phone and took the mouthpiece off and handed it to Mace.

When he had dialled he could hear the phone ringing at the other end. It rang a long time before he heard Hallet's voice, sounding tired and defensive.

'Hello James, I'm just about to go to see my friend. I wanted to check that you were still of a mind to see him.'

There was no answer from the other end and after a few moments Mace spoke again, urgently. 'James – are you there James, is anything the matter?'

There was still no answer and Mace looked across anxiously at Thorne who was about to speak when Mace suddenly held up his hand and listened intently. He could hear Hallet at the other end. He was sobbing and then Mace heard him say, 'My God, I just can't take any more I've had . . .' and there was the noise of the phone dropping and a cry. Mace called Hallet's name several times but there was no response and with obvious reluctance he hung up.

Mace had phoned the cottage again and the girl answered.

'How is Jimmy now, Kristina?'

'Not good but I speak to doctor.'

'What brought this on, have you any idea?'

'I think it a letter he got this morning.'

'Oh, what was it about?'

'It was from his attorney.'

'What did it say?'

'It said they heard from his wife's attorneys that she decided not to go ahead with the divorce.'

'Any reasons given?'

'No, no reasons said.'

'Anything else upset him?'

There was a long pause and then she said, 'I think the man who came in from the rain upset him.'

'How?'

'I don't know, I'm just guessing.'

'I see, well let me know what the doctor says and if you need anything phone me. I mean that.'

At the cottage the girl made two telephone calls. The second was to the operator asking to be put through to the nearest doctor. When he came he had examined Hallet

89

where he lay. Together they had got him to bed. The doctor gave him a shot of Valium, and sitting on the bed he turned to the girl.

'Well you'd better tell me what's been going on.'

'He's very worried — about a divorce and his work, I think that's the reason. He didn't sleep at all last night.'

'Well, that sounds enough. I've given him sufficient to keep him out for six or seven hours. He's to take these pills one every two hours and I'll call in again this evening.'

When the doctor had gone the girl dialled a London number and there was a click at the other end and a voice reciting 'The Lord's Prayer'. When it got to 'the power and the glory' she spoke into the mouthpiece and said, 'The keys are here. Message ends.'

Venturi's car had been spotted as it passed through Edenbridge. The patrol car had radioed the special number and the car's possible routes had been segmented. It finally slid to a gentle stop in the side road in Sanderstead. The Post Office van had seen Venturi leave the car and two hours later Farrow had set up a continuous surveillance. He had also warned Signals Security and just before mid-day they taped a twenty-second burst of high-speed Morse from Venturi's transmitter. They passed copies of the tapes to NSA through the CIA for their urgent assistance in de-coding. All that day there was a flow of radio traffic between Venturi, Moscow and Warsaw.

When the doctor called during the evening Hallet was still asleep, and the doctor checked his pulse and put a stethoscope to his chest. Then he stood up and turned to the girl. 'He must have been very low, very low indeed. I'll leave you two capsules for the night. When he wakes he'll be very muzzy and I'd like him to have some food. Some soup, something light.' He looked at her with raised eyebrows. 'Are you sure you can manage all right on your own like this?'

The girl nodded, 'Yes, I can manage doctor. Is he very ill?'

'He's in a bad state, there's no doubt about that. He needs lots of sleep and oblivion. That brain of his has been over-taxed. He's thinking to no purpose and that's bad for this kind of man. Needs rest and no responsibilities. I'm sure you'll be doing him good. Now call me if you need me. Don't hesitate, my dear.'

Hallet had not awoken and she had sat by his bed reading until 1 a.m. when her book had fallen from her hand and she had felt an overwhelming need to sleep herself. She decided to make herself a black coffee.

As she stepped down into the hall there was a man sitting facing the stairs. He was pointing a gun at her.

CHAPTER XIV

When Hallet woke he couldn't remember where he was and he lay near the surface of awareness like a half-submerged log, somewhere between sleeping and waking. His body felt heavy from the drug and the effort to move seemed too much. It was almost two hours before he sat up in the bed. He stood and walked unsteadily to the window, and as he pulled aside the curtains he saw the autumn sun lighting up the valley and he knew where he was. He was at the cottage. At Goudhurst.

There'd been the man in the rain and Martin at the table. And suddenly he remembered the girl. Her side of the bed was smooth and untouched and he listened. The house was still and empty and distant sounds were faint and echoing as they always are when a house is empty. Even as he called out he knew he was alone. There was a book which had fallen on the floor. A paperback anthology of Mary McCarthy. She must have been reading it. Getting to the door made him wet with perspiration and his legs shook as he made his way slowly downstairs.

On the table in the hall was a small pile of mail. Several of the letters were already opened and as he looked at them he realized he'd seen them before. But it seemed a long, long time ago. He remembered the one about the divorce. His hands trembled as he opened the others. An invitation to talk in Canterbury. A request for an interview by a local journalist. And then he saw the girl's round, careful, schoolgirl writing.

Dearest Jimmy,
     I have had to leave suddenly. I shall be staying for a few days at the Polish embassy. I understand you can phone me there.

                    All my love,
                         Kris

He sat on the chair in the hall for almost half an hour trying to make his brain function. Several times his hand reached for the telephone and each time it was withdrawn. All he wanted to do was to sleep again, and the thought of a soft bed and a pillow was hypnotic. Thoughts of the girl came flooding back and his anger gave him some small energy. He ran a warm bath and afterwards he had felt fresher and livelier. And after he had shaved and dressed he packed his bag and walked unsteadily out to the car. He was closing the door when the phone rang and he hurried back inside. It was Mace.

'Is that you James?'

'Yes it is Martin.'

'Are you feeling better now? I expected to speak to Kris.'

'She's gone Martin, she's gone.'

'Gone. Where, for God's sake?'

'She left a note. Said she was going to stay at the Polish embassy for a few days.'

'Why the Polish embassy? I thought she was Danish.'

'She is. It's all crazy. I think she's been kidnapped.'

'Oh nonsense James. Bloody embassies don't go round kidnapping foreign nationals. And if they did they wouldn't let their victims leave notes behind. It doesn't make sense. Are you coming up to London today?'

'I was on my way when you called.'

''Phone me as soon as you get here James.'

Hallet put back the receiver then lifted it and dialled Inquiries.

He spoke to the principal of the detective agency and arranged to see the two assistants at the Ebury Street flat.

Rogers's body was found at seven o'clock in the evening by a family on their way home from apple-picking. It lay face downwards at the edge of the orchard. It was early on the following day before it was identified and an emergency post-mortem gave no indication of the cause of death. Hallet's house was searched by a team from Special Branch but there was nothing of interest, and the supervision of the house and garden had been handed over to the local police.

The two private detectives listened to Hallet's story with

apparent indifference. They had learned over the years to listen and then divide their clients' stories by half and still check everything. Collet, the senior man, wore a modest dark-blue suit. He was a typical ex-detective sergeant of the kind that always seem to have chosen their suits with their minds on higher things. Collet bulged in most directions and the chair creaked ominously as he moved from time to time in apparent boredom. His colleague Dunn was younger. Sports-coated and casual he asked most of the questions. Then Collet put his large hand on Dunn's knee to silence him.

'Dr. Hallet, have you checked that Miss Olsen *is* at the embassy?'

'No. But I'm sure she is.'

Collet pursed his lips and nodded. I expect you're right but I'd like it checked. How about phoning now sir?'

Hallet reached for the phone and the directory. When he'd rung the number a man's voice answered. 'The Polish embassy, can I help you?'

'Yes I'd like to speak to Miss Olsen.'

'Miss who?' and then recognition. 'Ah, yes. Just a moment please.'

There were several clicks and then a voice speaking excellent English said, 'Is that Dr. Hallet?'

'Yes Hallet speaking.'

'Well I'm sorry, doctor, but she's not available at the moment. Shall I ask her to call you?'

'Yes please. Shall I let you know my movements?'

The voice at the other end held the shade of a smile, but it answered smoothly, 'No that won't be necessary. Thank you for calling doctor.' And the line had gone dead.

He saw Collet looking up expectantly and he nodded. 'Yes she's there. Or at least they acknowledge that she's there.'

Collet stood up and offered his hand to Hallet. 'We'll contact you early tomorrow morning Dr. Hallet.' It was rather a damp hand but so was the face and the bald head but Hallet had a feeling that these two knew what they were up to. He had said nothing about Omega Minus or Venturi.

* * *

Collet and Dunn were back at the flat by ten o'clock the next morning. Collet creaked his way into a chair and opened his notebook and flipped over the first few pages. Then he looked over at Hallet. 'Well the girl is there. We've seen her and I've no doubt she's a prisoner.'

'Can we prove this?'

Collet nodded his head. 'Yes we can. We've had photographs taken that show the girl at one of the windows. The window is barred. The embassy is being photographed now at hourly intervals.'

He jabbed a finger at his notebook. 'We shall give you a report of all movements at the Polish embassy until you instruct us to stop. We are prepared to swear our reports to a Commissioner for Oaths. That means they are suitable material for a court action.'

Hallet looked pleased. 'What do you suggest our next move should be?'

Collet spoke as if he had it all worked out. 'I understand you know Sir Martin Mace – that he's a friend of yours.'

'That's true.'

'Right. I suggest you telephone him and tell him that you are seeing your MP to ask for a question to be put down in the House today or tomorrow. Also tell him that you will be calling a press conference three days from today where you will furnish copies of our sworn reports and photographs.

'He will probably try to persuade you to wait for government action. I recommend you do not wait because they will do nothing. They won't want any diplomatic disturbance on behalf of a girl who isn't even a British national.'

Hallet smiled. 'I'm glad you're a man of action Mr Collet and I'll do what you recommend. What else are you going to do?'

'We're going to try to get a statement from one of the servants that they've seen the girl there. But that won't be easy. By the way sir, there are several people watching the embassy now. Two I recognize. They're both from Special Branch and they're very senior too. There are at least two others carrying out surveillance. Somebody's a bit touchy already because we've been spoken to by beat coppers on the grounds that we were loitering.'

'What did you say to them?'

'Oh we were firm but friendly. Now sir, we'll keep in touch and report to you every day about this time.'

Hallet realized he was not playing fair with Collet and Dunn. They didn't know the background of Omega Minus and they didn't know that three governments were interested in the events at top level.

Mace had advised caution but Hallet had gone ahead. He found action a relief for his tension. Any action was better than none.

As soon as the question to the Foreign Secretary had been tabled it had been spotted by the *Daily Express* lobby correspondent. He had got no change from the Foreign Office press office. The Danish embassy had sounded genuinely surprised and had taken down details. He had bulldozed his way through to the Polish Ambassador who had refused to comment. Finally he had phoned Hallet who had told him that he was calling a press conference the next day. The correspondent had taken a taxi round to Hallet's flat and had offered the full support of the Beaverbrook Press if he could have sight of the detectives' reports and the photographs then and there.

Slightly apprehensively, Hallet agreed, and the documents were photographed and the pictures copied. A photographer was to come later to take pictures of the flat and Hallet. The story broke in the next day's *Daily Express*. It covered most of the front page. The headline went 'REDS KIDNAP PLOT: POLES HOLD GIRL AT EMBASSY'.

The Polish press office phoned Beaverbrook Newspapers to complain, and were persuaded that the Ambassador should give an exclusive interview that evening, to the parliamentary correspondent of the *Evening Standard*.

CHAPTER XV

The result of the *Evening Standard* interview was on the front page in the second edition. There was a picture of the Ambassador from the files. They wouldn't allow a photographer on the embassy premises. The headline ran 'POLISH ENVOY DENIES KIDNAP CHARGE' and the text continued:

When I called at the Polish embassy in Mayfair's Weymouth Street, writes Charlton Ziegler, *Evening Standard* reporter, it was at the request of the Ambassador. The interview took place in his luxury apartment and Mr. Borowski, aged 59, was wearing the ribbons of the Papal Cross of Honour 'Pro Ecclesia et Pontifice' and the Order of Lenin, and he touched them absent-mindedly as we talked of the accusations made by Dr. Hallet, aged 43, concerning the kidnapping and detention of Miss Kristina Olsen, his close friend and constant companion.

During the course of our conversation Mr. Borowski said, 'There is no question of Miss Olsen being kidnapped; she is certainly here at the embassy and has asked for our protection. Who else will take responsibility for her?' When it was pointed out that Dr. Hallett had a team of private detectives keeping the embassy under surveillance the Ambassador said, 'I'm afraid Dr. Hallet is being melodramatic or he's been reading too many James Bond stories.' The Ambassador laughingly agreed that he had read all the Bond stories but had not yet seen the films.

When asked if it would be possible to interview Miss Olsen the Ambassador said, 'At this moment she is having tea with some of my staff and it would not be possible to disturb her. Maybe some other time.'

In reply to questions concerning Miss Olsen's freedom to come and go, Mr. Borowski stated, 'Of course she is free to come and go. She has been shopping almost every day I understand.' To questions regarding Miss Olsen's future movements he replied, 'It is a free world, no? She can do as she chooses. I think she hopes to go to Poland when this silly uproar is over.'

There was a report of 'No comment' from the Danish embassy and a Foreign Office spokesman said, 'The matter is under consideration. We can add nothing further.'

Ed Farrow read through the newspaper reports with Tad Anders. 'I like the bit about his Vatican ribbon, he must have got that when he was holed up in Vichy during the war.'

Anders smiled. 'All he's saying is "My dad's bigger than your dad". Take a look at that.'

'That' was a 'feedback' from NSA on monitored radio traffic between the Polish embassy and Moscow instructing the Poles to hold the girl at all costs. Protests by public and government could be attacked as imperialist, and otherwise ignored. There were to be no more interviews with the press. Statements were O.K. but no answers to questions.

By mid-day there were two TV teams outside the embassy and a crowd of reporters and photographers. At three o'clock His Excellency left by car for the Foreign Office where he had been ordered by Warsaw to make a formal protest. A leak from the Foreign Office had hinted at raised voices and threats of reprisals.

Hallet, looking drawn and haggard, was interviewed on ITN's early news. He confirmed that he was intending to marry Miss Olsen, that there had been no quarrel and that she had left no message. When questioned he stated that she had never shown any interest in politics or the Soviet Union. He admitted that he had not known that her mother was Russian. His comment that it was Communist blackmail was cut from the broadcast as going too far. But that section of the film clip wasn't destroyed.

The Soviet Ambassador had been summoned to the Foreign Office at 4 a.m. Fleet Street reckoned that the FO had checked on his return from a dinner at the Czech embassy, given him an hour to get to sleep and then demanded his immediate presence.

A junior official had given him a strong warning regarding the serious view taken by the FO of the abduction of the girl. He had refused to accept the rebuke and had left in a towering rage which was not improved when he caught sight of the Foreign Minister himself escorting the Finnish Consul in Hull to the head of the stairs. He took it as a deliberate snub. It was.

Parliament was a week into the new session and the Home Secretary was annoyed that what should be a Foreign Office affair had suddenly landed in his department. If you added the problem that the Chancellor of the Exchequer was also deeply involved there seemed all the makings of a first-class snarl up.

The Home Secretary's personal assistant came into the room and said, 'Sir Gwynn will be along in a moment. The PM is on the telephone.' Richard Thorne shuffled his papers with some irritation. He had come along prepared to take a back seat but it was so typical of the pompous little bugger to send in his P.A. with such a message. And there'd sure to be the fleeting reference to Llanelli defeating the All Blacks on Saturday to irritate the Honourable Member for Edinburgh, the Foreign Secretary.

Then Sir Gwynn came in looking suitably solemn. There had been a couple of introductions and the meeting had started. In addition to the three Cabinet ministers there were present Colonel Farrow SIS, Sir John Walker, D.Ops., SIS, Colonel Tadeusz Anders SIS, the Commissioner of Police, Sir Wentworth Woodhouse, a representative from the PM's office and a brace or two of senior civil servants from the three ministries concerned. The Home Secretary glanced around the table from under his ornate eyebrows and started the meeting.

'Good morning gentlemen. Thank you for assembling at such short notice. We have this problem as you know and it's finally ended up, as so many of these things do, on my department's plate. We have Sir Martin Mace and the two detectives outside in the anteroom and they are at our disposal if we think that is necessary.

'Now we have two situations really, one serious enough, the kidnapping of a Danish girl by the Poles and Russians which you will have read about in the press. But much more serious is the root of the trouble. Dr. James Hallet has discovered some infernal machine that appears to be of major interest to the Russians, the Americans, and, I must confess, to ourselves. We believe that the two things are closely connected. Dr. Hallet is interested in the girl and she is being used as a pressure point on him to give the details of his discovery to the Soviets. Now I'd like to ask the Foreign Secretary to outline the diplomatic aspects for us. Andrew – if you'd be so good.'

Andrew Maclean was the youngest of the three ministers present and at forty-nine gave an impression of casual efficiency which well suited the Foreign Office. He consulted no papers, did not look around the table, but rolled a gold pencil back and forth along the blotter in front of him.

'Our position is quite clear. Until somebody actually establishes a kidnapping or Miss Olsen indicates that she is being held against her will, no offence has been committed either diplomatic or civil.' There was some stirring around the table and although he disdained to look up he held up a white dead hand to hush the non-existent clamour.

'However,' and in case the portent of the word was not apparent first time round he said it again. 'However, we have applied unofficial pressure. We've had both the Polish and Russian ambassadors in and torn off a strip but we don't want to overdo it or our chaps in Warsaw and Moscow will merely get the same. If this fracas continues we can declare one or all of their diplomats "persona non grata" and they'll have to leave. They'd do the same to ours of course and my people estimate that it would cost us about £150,000 one way or another in re-location costs. The PM would have to make that decision of course.' Even at the end he didn't look up. He neither sought nor invited their approval of his views.

'Thank you Andrew. Now, Colonel Farrow, can you fill in your side for us.'

Anders looked across at Ed Farrow. It seemed strange to see him properly dressed for once. Blue suit, white shirt and a modest bow-tie.

'Well gentlemen. The girl was kidnapped from Hallet's

cottage in Kent and she's been held now for some days. We have photographs of her at one of the embassy windows. She has not been out since being taken there.'

'Just a moment colonel, I think Mr. Laidlaw of the FO wants to speak. Go ahead Mr. Laidlaw.'

'Through you, mister chairman, may I ask Colonel Farrow if he's sure she's not been out? The Polish Ambassador told the *Daily Express* that she'd been shopping every day.'

Farrow looked at the Home Secretary, who nodded.

'Mr. Laidlaw, the interview as printed and the journalist's notes quote the Ambassador as saying he "understood" she had been shopping every day. Put like that it is meaningless. He didn't even say she had been "out" shopping. He could come back and claim she had shopped on the phone. Anyway forget all that, take it from me the girl has not been out and she won't be going out until this whole thing is resolved. The Ambassador will tell any lie to suit himself – that's what ambassadors are for these days. Does that cover your point Mr. Laidlaw?' Laidlaw looked red in the face but he nodded, and Farrow continued.

'The whole thing hangs around an invention or some such thing that Hallet evolved. There are definite indications that it is a very significant weapon —' Again he was interrupted and it was Anders this time.

'Are we in the hydrogen bomb area or small arms?'

Farrow leaned back comfortably. 'I'm not sure, but I'd say in the hydrogen bomb area. Hallet himself seems very disturbed about it.'

The Chancellor chipped in, sharp-voiced. 'I have had some evaluation done on the few clues we have, and I think we have to face the fact that it is a fundamental weapon – a significant threat.' He looked back at Farrow who went on.

'I have had the embassy watched twenty-four hours a day. Hallet's two private detectives are covering most of the day and there are indications that others are concerned as well. I include the CIA. There has been very heavy signals traffic from the embassy to Warsaw and Moscow.

'It is in a very sophisticated code. Because of the urgency

101

we passed material to the CIA some time back with a request that NSA break the code for us. It would take us months. So far they have not been successful.

'The man Sergei Venturi is a very high-grade operator for the GRU – lots of experience. He was responsible for kidnapping the girl and for Rogers's death. He was holed up in a house in Sanderstead which we recently put under surveillance. We think he spotted the surveillance. Anyway he abandoned the house and is now at the Polish embassy. We have no record of his entry to the UK, either as a civilian, tourist or diplomat.

'Hallet will not at this stage discuss his discovery with anyone, not even Sir Martin who is a very close friend. My greatest worry is that someone on the other side will decide that the best solution is to kill Hallet and let his secret die with him. At the moment I don't think this is the Russian view. In nuclear armament they are tactically slightly behind the West at the moment, and I think they would prefer to have a go at getting Hallet's weapon before resorting to wiping him out.

'I have put a guard on Hallet but he is a difficult man. He won't co-operate except on his own terms and conditions, and quite frankly he's so naïve he doesn't realize what deep waters he's in.

'At the moment I'm concentrating on protecting Hallet, preventing him from giving his secret to a foreign government and keeping the general situation from boiling over. I should like to be able to spend more time with Hallet in the hope of persuading him at the right moment to tell us what he has discovered. And to that end I should like to ask for my resources to be increased immediately.'

The Home Secretary nodded approvingly. 'Thank you colonel. Sir John and I will have words about extra resources for you. Had you anything particular in mind?'

'Yes sir. I'd like Colonel Anders and his team full-time, and I'd like a Signals Security detachment full-time.'

'Right, we'll see what we can do. Well, gentlemen, I'll call another meeting as soon as it is necessary.'

There was no doubt that Farrow would get the help he asked for and Anders joined him as he walked from the room. Sir Martin came across immediately. He looked very agitated.

'Mister Farrow, Colonel Farrow, I must talk to you urgently.'

Farrow introduced Anders and Sir Martin put his hand in his inside jacket pocket and pulled out an envelope. As he handed it to Farrow he said, 'It came this morning colonel. They must be mad or desperate, one or the other.'

Farrow took out a card which was inside and checked that there was nothing else inside the envelope. Then he looked carefully at the postcard-sized photograph. Anders looked too. Farrow looked up. 'Thank you Sir Martin. Please don't mention this to anyone – not Hallet, or the press or anyone. I can make best use of it if we keep it to ourselves.' He turned to Anders. 'Tad, I'm going to Hallet straight away. When I come back I'd like a blow-up of the face of the man facing the camera. Cut out the rest of the picture. See if any of our FO boys or Special Branch can identify the man.'

CHAPTER XVI

'There's no doubt, Dr. Hallet, that the girl's mother was Russian. I've seen her birth certificate, marriage certificate and her passport. Another thing that was noticed in our check was that the Russians very quickly let the matter of the mother's defection settle into obscurity. They don't normally give up that easily. We have also checked in the Soviet Union that Mrs. Olsen's relatives were not punished or disturbed in any way. That in itself is significant. There are other points concerning this business of yours where it is quite clear that the Russians are better informed than we are and there is a strong indication that the information must have come from someone very close to you. And at the moment that can only be Miss Olsen.'

Farrow felt sorry for Hallet. He was punch-drunk but he was trying to look alert, and indeed anger and surprise had kept his adrenalin flowing in the last few days. Hallet said nothing and Farrow continued,

'As you know, we feel that the Russians planted the girl on you and I'd like to go over that aspect in detail with you.' He looked questioningly at Hallet who gritted his teeth and then nodded. 'All right Mr. Farrow.'

Farrow looked questioningly at Hallet. 'Let me say, Dr. Hallet, that we are taking for granted that you want us to contact the girl and give her protection if she does need it?'

Hallet nodded quickly, 'That's so Mr. Farrow.'

'Now, you met her at the bookshop at Grand Central.'

'Yes.'

'Had you planned to go there?'

'No.'

'When did you decide to go?'

'While I was looking at the exhibition at the Guggenheim.'

'You were alone?'

'Yes.'

'Was the girl there at the bookshop when you arrived?'

'I don't think so. I didn't notice her.'

Farrow smiled at Hallet. 'I think she's too attractive for either of us not to notice and there is really nowhere that provides cover inside the shop, is there?'

'No. I don't remember any.'

'I have had it checked, doctor. There's no cover inside.' He wanted to see if Hallet pursued the matter but he didn't.

'You've already put what happened about the book in your statement so I'll go on to another area.' He looked across to Hallet and his eyes were watching every movement of Hallet's eyes and mouth. 'Dr. Hallet, at what point did you and Miss Olsen first have sexual intercourse?' Hallet tried to look away but in the end his eyes came back and he said in a low voice, 'The first day.'

'Where?'

'At my apartment.'

'Dr. Hallet, I know that well-known men have more sexual opportunities than the rest of us but did this incident not surprise you?'

'You mean a girl going to bed the first day?'

'No, that's been done before. I mean this particular girl. She is very young, extremely pretty, a quite outstanding creature. Did it not strike you in any way as suspicious? Not in the sense we are discussing now but perhaps that she might be after your money.'

Hallet's look was slightly supercilious. 'Mr. Farrow, if she had been after my money I should not have been suspicious. I can well afford to pay, so I was not suspicious on that account. I expect you think I should have been suspicious that such a pretty girl, so much younger than I, should have gone to bed with *me* so quickly. Is that it?'

Farrow didn't look abashed, he just nodded. 'Yes, that's it.'

'No, I wasn't suspicious, I just thought I was very lucky, and I still do. And I don't believe it *was* suspicious.'

Farrow looked at Hallet for a long time and then he said, 'Did you get tired of the girl sexually?'

'No.'

'So you want her back?'

Hallet flushed with anger. 'I'm going to marry Miss Olsen as soon as it is possible. This is insulting.'

Farrow cut in. 'Let's go back to the Guggenheim. How did you go there?'

'I walked.'

'Quite a walk from your apartment.'

Hallet looked uneasy and didn't speak.

'Maybe you didn't walk from your apartment. Is that it?'

Hallet nodded.

'Where did you walk from?'

'A friend's apartment.'

'Man or woman?'

'A girl.'

'Where was her apartment?'

'On East 59th.'

'What was the girl's name?'

'Jackie.'

'Jackie what?'

'I've no idea.'

Farrow looked long and hard and finally Hallet said, 'She was a call-girl.'

'You stayed all night there?'

'Yes.'

Farrow took down the call-girl's address and then went back to his questions.

'Had you any previous appointments for the Sunday?'

'I don't think so. I'd planned a free day on my own.'

'And you decided to go to the bookshop at Grand Central while you were in the exhibition.'

'Yes.'

'Why?'

'I realized I had nothing to read. Nothing light that is.'

'So you came out and then what?'

'I hailed a taxi and went to Grand Central.'

'Just a minute Dr. Hallet. Was the taxi waiting outside the gallery?'

'No, I saw it coming and waved.'

'Anyone else wave?'

'I seem to remember a couple of ladies waving.'

106

'But the taxi took you.'

'Yes.'

'You didn't think this was odd?'

'No, not really. Just lucky.'

Girls, taxis, this man really believes in luck, thought Farrow. He leafed through the pages of his notebook.

'Dr. Hallet, why do *you* think the girl has gone to the Polish embassy?'

Hallet shrugged. 'I've no idea Mr. Farrow. No idea at all. At first I thought maybe she was frightened of you people.'

Farrow looked surprised. 'Me?'

'Well the secret service, whatever it's called, MI5 maybe.'

The pattern was clearer now and Farrow saw that the Russians must have had the girl in reserve waiting an opportunity to pick up Hallet. From then on they'd relied on Hallet's lust. They'd been right.

'Dr. Hallet, during your time with the girl has she given any indication at all that she has any connection with the Soviets? Even the slightest indication.'

'Like what?'

Farrow shrugged and smiled. 'Oh there could be a dozen ways. For instance, does she play chess like a Russian?' He saw Hallet's face go pale and he followed through.

'Well Dr. Hallet?'

'We never played chess.'

Farrow flung his file on the table and stood up, leaning over Hallet, angry and on the point of violence.

'Don't play silly buggers with me, Hallet, or I'll have you inside on suspicion.'

'Suspicion of what Mr. Farrow? Sleeping with a girl whose mother was born Russian? Come, come, you'll have to do better than that.'

There were white patches on Farrow's cheeks and his mouth looked grim and his hand went for Hallet's throat. It caught up his shirt and his tie and he shook Hallet in his seat. He could hardly speak for his anger.

'Hallet you've got half the security forces of this country tied up because we are trying to play democrats with you. It may be fun to you or you may be indifferent, but it's bloody serious to me. It's serious for that blonde of yours

107

too. So are you going to answer my questions or do I get rough?'

Hallet was trembling as he said, 'It's you who's doing the harm Farrow. The girl will be all right.'

Farrow shoved Hallet back in the chair and turned angrily to the file on the table. He took out an envelope and pushed it across to Hallet. 'Right Hallet, take a look at that. Look carefully. Look at the date on the postmark first.'

He watched as Hallet looked at the envelope. The postmark was Central London and the date was the day before. Hallet took out the card inside and looked at it. Then he looked up at Farrow. He was shaking and at the point of collapse. 'How can I help? Tell me?' And he put his head in his hands and sobbed.

Farrow glanced again at the photograph. It was a Polaroid colour print and it showed the girl and two men. She was naked and one of the men was holding her arm in an agonizing lift behind her back. Her body was arched backwards to try to ease the pain. The other man had his hand between the girl's legs.

CHAPTER XVII

The envelope was addressed to Sir Martin Mace at the current address of SIS.

Farrow waited for Hallet to recover and then he said, 'Hallet I want you to listen carefully.'

Hallet nodded his eager agreement.

'Does the word or words Omega Minus mean anything to you?'

Hallet hesitated but only for a second. 'Yes, it does.'

'Can you tell me what it is?'

'It's a code to lock data into a computer.'

'Is this to do with your discovery?'

'Yes.'

'Have you given this codeword to anybody?'

'No – definitely not.'

'Not to us. Not to Sir Martin for instance?'

'No, not to anyone.'

'We have monitored certain Russian transmissions in code and I have to inform you that that codeword is known to them.'

'That's impossible – absolutely impossible.'

Farrow tried to be patient. 'Let's go back to where we were, Dr. Hallet. I asked you if there was anything that gave even a slight indication of a Russian connection with the girl. I cited playing chess like a Russian and I had the impression that this reminded you of something. Am I right?'

Hallet nodded. 'Yes. On the very first day she recognized a piece of Russian music that's not very well known and she remembered the composer's name.'

'Is she interested in music?'

'She likes music but isn't really interested I would say.'

'O.K. Now back to this codeword Omega Minus. Tell me about it.'

'It's just that. A codeword. I wrote a small piece of computer programming so that a whole data bank of information could only be accessed by using this codeword. It was also a check word. I could use a certain code and if it turned up Omega Minus on the display screen it indicated that nobody else had accessed the data bank.'

'Does the data bank give all the details of your discovery?'

'Not in a coherent form. It is all there but it doesn't hang together.'

'I'm sorry I don't understand.'

'Well, if you take a decent dictionary there's a Shakespeare play in it. But you need to sort the words first. That's roughly what I mean.'

'So even an expert couldn't put it together even if he got access to this material in the computer?'

'Probably a code-breaker and a scientist working together could do this.'

'And then they've got your weapon?'

'No, not at all. And it's not a weapon in the way you imagine it. It's a device that changes a natural law, temporarily, and that can do damage.'

'To people?'

'Yes. But not like a weapon does damage.'

'But you must require a means to cause this alteration. An appliance, a machine, something like that.'

Hallet nodded. 'That's true.'

'And I assume that you have made such an appliance.'

Hallet looked up at Farrow and was silent for what seemed a long time. 'Yes, I made one.'

'And that's what caused the trouble on *Pillager* and the FE-111E.'

Hallet nodded. 'Yes I'm afraid so.'

'Where is the thing now?'

'I don't want to say. Not yet anyway.'

'You realize that if you were kidnapped you would be forced to talk. That's what the girl's kidnapping is all about.'

'It seems they are more perceptive than your people.'

'I don't understand. In what way?'

'If the girl was just a sleeping partner they'd know the pressure wouldn't work. At least they think I care – that I love her.'

'Maybe you're right, but that won't stop them from using the girl.'

'But you obviously think she's on their side. That she works for them.'

Farrow laughed harshly. 'If you think that will stop them from hurting her or killing her you just don't know the Russians. Can we go back a bit Dr. Hallet? You said it was impossible for the Russians to have learnt the code-word. Now we already know that that isn't true. We learnt it from them. Any ideas?'

'I wrote the programme personally. Nobody else has ever had access to the computer, or its data bank. I've never discussed the codeword with anyone.'

'What about Sir Martin Mace? Have you discussed it with him?'

'As vaguely as I've discussed it with you Mr. Farrow. I've never mentioned the codeword.'

'What about Miss Olsen?'

'I've never mentioned the codeword to her but I once used it on the VDU when she was in my office. But she wouldn't know what it was.'

'Did she ask what you were doing?'

'No.'

Farrow stood up and picked up his file from the table. 'We're going to put pressure on the Polish embassy to get the girl released and it's almost certain that they will con-sider having a go at you.'

'You mean kidnapping me?'

'Not necessarily. They might be satisfied with killing you.'

'What good would that do?'

'Well if you hadn't told anyone of your device it would mean we should all go back to square one.'

Farrow waited, but Hallet said nothing, and Farrow went on, 'You realize that telling me or Sir Martin, or someone else whom you trust would act as an insurance for you, and maybe for the girl.'

'You mean because they'd know that if they killed me it wasn't the end of Omega Minus?'

'Precisely.'

Hallet stood up slowly and walked over to the window.

After a few moments he turned to face Farrow. 'I'm sorry Mr. Farrow but I'm not prepared to talk further about Omega Minus but I'll see that there's information left for you if I feel I'm getting into deeper waters than I can cope with.'

CHAPTER XVIII

The story stayed on the front pages and was a continuing theme on radio and TV. For several days after the story had broken there were continuous crowds of sightseers gathered outside the embassy. There was nothing to see apart from camera crews, photographers and journalists. Finally the police erected barriers at both ends of Weymouth Street and only residents were allowed free passage along with visitors including those members of the press who passed some unstated Metropolitan Police requirements.

Farrow had taken over the top floor of a house used by a medical consortium and there were cameras and TV cameras trained on the main door and the general structure of the Polish embassy. The girl had not been seen since the photographs obtained by the detectives had been published in the dailies.

Ambassador Borowski was not yet used to a diplomatic life with a background of harassment, but he doggedly kept some appointments. In the early days of the siege he had lashed out at a photographer and had been loudly booed by the crowd. He was not used to this other side of democracy and he took the rabble of newspaper men as acting under government orders. He had driven the two press secretaries mad as they tried to persuade him that he would improve his image if he would only grin and bear it.

He and the Soviet Ambassador had delivered countless protests from their governments concerning harassment and aggressive behaviour. They were received with patient charm by young men who gave the impression that this was merely part of their training. Moscow and Warsaw were not playing it cool and there was a flood of orders and counter-orders.

The man in the photograph twisting the girl's arm had been identified and at that point the Foreign Secretary called for the Polish Ambassador and the Soviet Ambassador to attend at a joint meeting at the Foreign Office. It was timed for nine o'clock in the evening.

The ambassadors arrived together in the same car and were shown up immediately to the Minister's rooms. They had discussed the current position on the journey and they assumed there was to be some kind of deal. This was Moscow's view also, and their instructions had been to be cool and noncommittal.

Their coats and hats were taken by a secretary and they were shown into the Minister's reception room. Andrew Maclean stood grim-faced behind his desk. On their side the usual brocade-covered chairs had been removed. They had been given no choice but to stand. There was no proffered hand and he looked coolly at each of them in turn. Maclean then read from a paper which he held in his hand.

'Your Excellencies, I am instructed to inform you that Her Majesty's Government is now in possession of positive evidence that you are holding Miss Kristina Olsen at your embassy premises in Weymouth Street, Mayfair against her will. I have to inform you that unless Miss Olsen is released forthwith Her Majesty's Government will consider what action to take to ensure her release.'

Maclean put the paper carefully back on his desk and looked at his watch as if noting the exact time when the information had been given.

Borowski smelled trouble but he knew that he had to find out more. 'Minister, I cannot accept this rebuke from Her Majesty's Government and I can only assume that, in the unlikely event that you had such evidence, you would have indicated what this evidence might be.'

Andrew Maclean had expected denials and hedgings but when they came they were too much for him and as he pushed forward the photograph he roared, 'There, Mister Ambassador of Poland – there's the evidence. Take a good look.'

Both ambassadors leaned forward to look at the photograph. The Soviet Ambassador knew nothing of it at all and had never seen the girl. But Borowski recognized the girl and the men. He hadn't been informed about it by Ven-

114

turi but he could even identify the wallpaper in the room the girl was held in. He stood up and looked at Maclean.

'Minister I don't know what this is all about. You send for us. You make accusations and threats and now you show me a pornographic picture as evidence. Evidence of what?'

'You recognize the girl, Borowski, or are you denying that?'

'Of course I recognize her, it is Miss Olsen, but what has that to do with me?'

'That photograph was taken in your embassy and sent to Dr. Hallet.'

Borowski shrugged. 'How can we tell where it was taken or why? I have heard that Dr. Hallet is very active sexually. Maybe he can explain to us.'

'There is nothing to explain Borowski. The man behind the girl is named Pawel Stretzki and he is an accredited member of your staff. Came here seventeen months ago. Position designated as assistant motor mechanic. In fact he's a member of your security service – a captain in Z-11.' He paused only to draw breath. 'And I warn you if that bastard puts his nose outside your embassy we'll have him, and his feet won't touch.'

Andrew Maclean could hear his own angry, undiplomatic words ringing in his ears. There was something about the photograph and the thinking behind it that especially offended his fastidious Edinburgh upbringing. Lust was understandable and most men could enjoy having a hand between that young lovely's legs. But it wasn't lust. It was cold and contrived. Worked out to put pressure on a jealous man. He realized Borowski was speaking again.

'. . . and I am certain that my Government will not accept your so-called evidence.'

Maclean put both hands on the table and leaned forward towards the two men.

'Borowski. If I have to I'll have that photograph printed in every paper in the UK with a full explanation. And alongside it I'll get them to put the passport photo we have on our records when you applied for Stretzki to enter the UK. I have no doubt whom the people will believe and

I would not like to be you if you try to leave your embassy that day or any day afterwards.'

Lynsky, the Soviet Ambassador, had been in the business much longer than his Polish colleague and he preferred the diplomatic niceties. He had never seen a British Foreign Secretary so heated and abusive before. Cold, hard, frostbitten yes, but shouting and table-pounding never.

'Minister, I note what you have to say and although I am not sure why I have been asked here with His Excellency the Polish Ambassador I do suggest that all concerned take time to work out a proper solution.'

Even this was not enough to avert the lightning, it seemed, for Maclean turned and looked at him angrily. 'Your Excellency is here because your Government is involved – deeply involved. And I refer to Sergei Venturi who is a Soviet national, a senior officer in the GRU, now at the Polish embassy controlling the affair of the girl.'

Lynsky was still cool as he replied. 'I find it inexplicable, Minister, that you are seeing the ambassadors of two independent but friendly nations together. I cannot understand why.'

'I'll tell you why Lynsky. It's a courtesy. If I'm going to shoot the monkey I like to tell the organ-grinder first.'

That was enough for Lynsky. He bowed and walked away. When he had had a moment to realize what was going on Borowski followed him.

CHAPTER XIX

Hallet was alone in the Ebury Street flat. It was the day after the two ambassadors had been jointly called to the Foreign Office. Hallet was waiting for Farrow. Somehow Farrow had seemed to become a friend. At least he was someone actively doing something to help the girl, someone who knew all the background and at least overtly passed no judgements on Hallet's behaviour. The newspapers and broadcasters obviously had no idea why the girl had been captured, and they had gradually ceased to contact Hallet, because the girl and Whitehall became the focus of their attentions. Farrow had insisted that Collet and Dunn be paid off and Farrow was now Hallet's only link with the action. Sir Martin Mace had been warned off by Farrow who wanted Hallet to end up with only one person to confide in.

As Hallet stood at the window he saw Farrow walking up Ebury Street and the incongruity of the whole situation struck him. This man, grey, crew-cut hair, raincoat unbuttoned and flying out as he walked so briskly to his meeting. The tanned face intent and observant as it glanced at passers-by in the street. Then Farrow was looking up at the window and Hallet waved. Farrow smiled and nodded, and moments later the door-bell rang.

Farrow hung his raincoat carefully in the hallway and briefly put his hand to his short hair. He sat down, and Hallet sat too. Farrow looked across at Hallet and was surprised at the change in the man's appearance. The eyes were deep-set now, with bruise-coloured patches below them. There was a white ridge of fatigue each side of his mouth and the cheeks were concave. There was a clear indication of a skull below the drawn flesh.

Although it was nearly noon Hallet was still wearing pyjamas under his tartan dressing-gown. There was a half-empty bottle of Dewars' on the table and the stale rem-

117

nants of a meal. Still looking hard at Hallet's face Farrow said,

'Why don't you let me fix a safe place for you? Somewhere where you can have proper attention. You need to eat a bit more. The girl is going to need looking after when we get her out and you'll need to be fit.'

Tears trembled at the edges of Hallet's eyes, and hung for a second before they rolled down his cheeks. He nodded but he couldn't speak. He wasn't used to any sort of kindness.

Farrow stood up and for the next ten minutes he cleared the table, washed up the dishes in the small kitchen and vacuumed the sitting-room carpet. These chores finished he sat down again.

Hallet smiled a watery smile. 'I guess I'm the only man in the country today who's had his housework done by a colonel in the secret service.'

Farrow smiled back. 'Keeping things ship-shape keeps up the morale. Keeps up mine anyway.'

'I can't imagine your morale ever needing to be kept up colonel.'

'And I couldn't invent anything doctor.'

'Are you married?'

'I was.'

'Divorced?'

'No, my wife and my boy were killed by a car a long time ago.'

'And you haven't wanted to marry anyone else?'

'Yes I have actually, but she was killed too.'

'How did it happen?'

'She was Russian, Georgian to be exact. Much younger than me. Very pretty, very alive, and we were going to be married. I was operating in Berlin at the time. I was due a month's leave in three weeks' time and we were going to be married then. The Russians had her killed. Now, let's get back to our problem.'

Hallet interrupted. 'I'm very sorry colonel, truly sorry. I'd no idea when I asked.'

'Have you kept to my instructions regarding Venturi?'

'Yes. I've not contacted him and for that matter he's not tried to contact me.'

118

Farrow shook his head. 'Oh he's tried to contact you all right. We have an intercept on your phone and your mail, and there's a plain-clothes man patrolling in Ebury Street – Venturi has tried to contact you every day.'

Then Farrow told Hallet most of what had gone on at the Foreign Office interview the previous evening.

'And will the Government take these steps?'

'No doubt about it.'

'What will the Poles do?'

'I'm not certain but my estimate is that they won't back down. There's going to be a lot of trouble. Meantime I'd like your help.'

'What can I do?'

'I want you to phone Venturi at the Polish embassy and tell him that you will do a deal for the release of the girl. I want you to phone from a public call box, not from here. Let him know that it's a public phone. Tell him that you will tell him where one of your devices is. Say that it's inaccessible but can be salvaged. Use the word salvage and he'll begin to hook on. Tell him you want a reply today. Whatever he offers, whatever he says, don't say anything beyond what I have said. O.K?'

Hallet nodded. 'And what do I tell him if he agrees?'

Farrow shook his head. 'He won't agree, he can't, he'll have to ask Moscow. He'll make some arrangement to contact you. If he even hinted that he agreed then and there, you'll know he's trying to con you. Just hang up.'

Hallet looked pleased and Farrow was sorry that he had to be deceived. 'I'll go and get dressed. How shall I contact you to let you know what happens?'

'Oh just dial the number I gave you. They'll contact me wherever I am.'

It was nearly an hour later when Hallet spoke to Farrow.

'I spoke to Venturi, colonel. You were quite right, he said he would have to consult Moscow. He seemed very eager himself. He asked me to hang on a few moments then he came back and gave me some details. Shall I read them to you, I copied them down?'

'Yes please, go ahead.'

'I have to tune to a radio station called "Peace and

119

Progress". They have a broadcast in French at six o'clock tonight and right at the beginning they will mention a telephone number and if there are two threes in the number they agree and I should phone Venturi immediately. The station is on nineteen metres a frequency of . . .'

Farrow interrupted. 'Yes that's O.K. doctor. I know the frequency. That's fine, you just go ahead and do that. They'll say yes all right, I've no doubt about that.'

'And if they say yes and I phone Venturi, what do I tell him?'

'Tell him that Omega Minus was on a raft being towed by a navy tug on the night of 24 July.'

'What else do I tell him? Won't they want to know what happened to the platform, or where the *Pillager* was at the time?'

Farrow laughed. 'No doctor they'll know. You don't give them any other information but you do try and find out when they will release the girl. Venturi will stall and say that he has to check on what you say. Argue a bit if you like but don't worry — it makes no difference to the outcome.'

Farrow was tuned to the frequency from five o'clock onwards and at a few seconds before six o'clock he heard the musical call-sign of two clarinets and then 'Ici l'émetteur "Paix et Progrès", la voix de l'opinion publique soviétique.' A few minutes later they mentioned their telephone number for visitors to Moscow. They repeated it three times. It was Moscow 2336465.

He reached for his phone and called Hallet.

'Did you hear the broadcast Dr. Hallett?'

'Yes I did, but on my set it was very faint.'

'Don't worry, it was what was expected. I'd like you to go out now and call Venturi from a different box. Phone me when you've finished.'

Somebody once said that there are few things to beat lying on a good bunk, in your own boat, reading a book, while sipping a malt whisky and listening to the rain on the coach-house roof. It had just stopped raining and a pale sun was laying a yellow gold sheen on the dirty Thames water. Farrow had taken down the canopy over the cockpit and after pouring a whisky had gone up the companionway to the comfortable seats in the fresh air.

He hadn't told anyone of his plan because he was not sure of what he was doing. All through this affair, right from the start, there had been something odd, something that didn't fit. He had a hunch now that he knew what it was. If he was right it would cause even more tension but at least they would know what they were up against. If he was wrong he would have wasted two or possibly three days and the situation would be at explosion point.

A River Police launch foamed past and the helmsman gave him a wave. As he raised his arm to return the wave the phone rang and he hurried down into the saloon. It was Hallet.

'I passed the information to Venturi. He asked where I was phoning from and I'm pretty sure he kept me talking deliberately and sent someone to check on where I was. I asked about when Kristina would be released and he said it would have to be after they had checked on the information and had found the device. He asked how they would recognize it and I refused to give any details.'

'Fine doctor, you've done very well. Now what are you doing this evening?'

'Nothing at all. I'm just waiting. I don't seem to be able to concentrate on anything so I just sit around.'

'Fair enough. Now do you know where Cadogan Pier is?'

'Isn't that the pier at Cheyne Walk?'

'That's it. Now how about taking a walk down to Cadogan Pier. You'll find a nice-looking boat there called *My Joanna*. I'll be on board and we'll have a meal together.'

Hallet sounded pleased. 'That would be very nice colonel. I'll get on my way.'

Farrow sat thinking, his hand still on the telephone. Then he dialled the number of Jake Salis. Jake Salis was the CIA man who liaised in London with SIS. He was a Texan and somebody had once said 'Jake Salis talks with that Texan drawl but you watch his eyes and you can see his mind going ten times as fast.'

Salis answered after a few rings, and Farrow spoke without any particular urgency.

'Have you had any news from Langley or Fort George Meade on the transmissions from the Polish embassy here Jake?'

'No Ed. They don't seem to be coming along with that stuff at all.'

'Can you have another push for us Jake? That stuff could help us a lot with these present troubles of ours.'

'I can see that Ed. Leave it with me and I'll see what I can do.'

Hallet had not eaten much but he seemed much more relaxed as they sat at the table in the saloon. He had talked about his work at Cambridge and then about his discovery of 'Plasticond'. Farrow had made a good audience. An intelligent but non-specialist listener. Hallet had one elbow on the table his hand cradling his chin, his head on one side. As he moved his wine-glass with the other hand he said very quietly, 'I'd find it a help if you'd let me tell you about this new thing.' Farrow nodded, but he didn't say anything.

'I'd been looking at reports of current research in Europe, and it was so obvious that no country had a planned programme of research in any field. I wondered if it was possible to write a programme that would indicate natural progressions for research. So I started with "Plasticond" as a base. As you know that was based on the fact that, explained crudely, in some material's atomic structure there is an apparently spare neutron, and this is what gives the material conductivity. I felt it would be possible to create an atomic structure in other materials – man-made materials for instance – that would also have this spare neutron and therefore be highly conductive.

'So the first thing to look at in my new computer programme was the opposite. Obviously the opposite of conductivity is insulation. On the whole, insulation is not very variable – generally a material either insulates or it doesn't. But I looked casually at the atomic structure of insulating materials – I mean electrical insulation of course.' Hallet looked across the table at Farrow. 'Is this boring you?'

122

Farrow smiled wryly and shook his head.

'I played about with this mathematically and it resolved itself quite easily. There was no possible need for making insulators non-insulating so I got on with working out the rest of the computer programme. But I found I kept coming back to these insulators, and for want of any other inspiration I played around with variable insulation – making an insulator capable of varying its insulating ability. Now in doing this I logically arrived at a formula that produced such reduced insulation that the material was impracticable as an insulator. The same calculation continued until I had arrived at negative insulation. In other words the insulator ceased to insulate, it became a conductor. It all centres around this spare, useless neutron again. And then something clicked and I went back to my notes on the plastic conductor and there it was. There was a radio frequency that could make this spare neutron positive or negative. It was at that point I realized that this was commercially and industrially useless but as a weapon it could grind a country to a halt in minutes.

'With a small, very simple, two frequency transmitter, you could wipe out the insulation on anything from a power station to a radio set. Cables, wires, insulation would all break down and there would be a series of short-circuits probably ending in fire. If the thing affected was mobile – a plane, a car, a train, it would cause loss of life.

'Despite this I pursued the matter until it took up all my time. In the end I built a small transmitter that would eliminate anything it was set for. In other words it could be aimed at a particular house or building. That doesn't sound much until I say that I mean a particular house anywhere. There is no wandering of the radio frequency so if we are here on this boat and you can give me the bearing of a house in Moscow and its precise distance, then we could set the transmitter and everything electrical in that house from mains cables to TV breaks down electrically and you've got fire and explosion. Train it on a battleship and the steering, gunnery, radar, everything, is done for. You can make the beam as fine as a laser or you can leave it on coarse pitch and wipe out towns and

123

cities. On coarse setting it only covers one degree but set it for fifteen hundred miles distance and sitting here at the table we just take a bearing of about six degrees magnetic and we wipe out the whole of Moscow.

'There's one difficulty I have with it at the moment but I won't go into that.'

Farrow pursed his lips. 'That's the error that wrecked the FE-111E.'

Hallet looked amazed. 'My God, how did you guess that? How could you possibly know?'

Farrow got up from the table and reached in one of the cupboards for another bottle.

'I didn't guess Dr. Hallet. Your device, as you say, can be set on any bearing. It was set on the known bearing for the target raft on *Pillager* on the night you were doing the Ministry of Defence tests. RAF Boulmer and the Royal Navy were testing out your modified metering device. You were carrying out another test in parallel. They didn't know about that. Your test caused a blasting short on the platform at the moment the rating got on to it. The thing you didn't know till later was that you'd wrecked the FE-111E because your device not only projects forwards on the set bearing but backwards on the reciprocal. The plane just happened to be in the wrong place at the wrong moment.'

Hallet nodded his head. 'Yes, that's right, that's what happened. Can you understand what I feel about this thing?'

'Yes, I can understand all right. Any country that has it *can* blackmail the others, I've no doubt about that. Part of you wishes you had never thought of it, or pursued it – but part of you can't bear to forgo impressing your fellow scientists.'

Hallet looked up quickly. 'I'm afraid that's true colonel. It sounds terrible but that's what's been tearing me up.'

'Try this, it's a malt whisky, it'll help you sleep.'

'What do we do now?'

'You don't do anything. You've done your part this evening. My job is to protect you, and to get the girl out safely. Changing the subject, I had a word with your wife and her solicitor. Your divorce is back on the list. I'd say it will be heard in about four weeks. The Treasury Solicitor tells me that undefended cases are now going through on time.'

Farrow walked with Hallet to Chelsea Bridge and then turned back for the boat.

He phoned Tad Anders at Central Intelligence.

'Tad I'd like a check on all Russian ships that approach the Northumberland coast in the next seven days. Say between parallel 55 and parallel 56.'

'O.K., hang on and I'll check out the current position.'

There was a gap of two or three minutes before Anders came on again.

'Ed, there is already a vessel on the move between those two parallels. She's doing an estimated 20 knots, going due west about 80 miles east of Tynemouth.'

'Who is she?'

'Our old friend the *Pyotr Illyich*. Is she what you were looking for?'

Farrow laughed. 'Yes, she suits me fine. I'll ring again tomorrow morning.'

The next morning Anders's news was beginning to make sense of some of the problem areas. The Russian spy boat *Pyotr Illyich* was now at the exact spot where the raft from *Pillager* had sunk. The captain of a civil airliner flying from Oslo to Newcastle had reported that the Russian vessel had divers operating. And during the night a United States nuclear submarine had left its station off the Orkney Islands and had travelled underwater at its full rated speed and was now standing off from the Russian ship. She was only a mile away, submerged and indulging in heavy radio traffic in code. Admiralty Intelligence had also noted these events and in its sitrep to Joint Intelligence had remarked that this was the first occasion in ten years that the Americans had allowed a nuclear sub to come nearer to a Russian electronics ship than ten miles.

Farrow spoke to the duty officer at the Joint Chiefs of Staff Office and gave reasons why undue surveillance would be unnecessary and disadvantageous.

CHAPTER XX

Anders invited Jake Salis to a meeting at one of the SIS offices on the top floor of the Passport Office in Petty France. He had not mentioned that Farrow was to be there and he was discussing a joint SIS–CIA operation in Toronto when Farrow came in. Salis had met Farrow on many occasions so he nodded affably as Farrow joined them at the circular white table.

Farrow exchanged a quick look with Anders and then putting his hands in his pockets rather defensively he looked at Salis and said, 'Jake, why are your people holding out on us about this signals traffic we've asked for your help on?'

Salis shrugged. 'Well you boys know the score as well as I do. The NSA deal with this for the CIA. We're in their hands and if they don't come across, well that's it. I keep pushing but it doesn't work.'

'Jake that's all very well but this stuff is top priority for us. There must be some reason why it isn't top priority for CIA.'

'What makes you think it isn't top priority for the CIA?'

'Because we haven't had a sniff out of them and they've had this for weeks.'

'So the boys haven't cracked a code, or they haven't got around to it.'

'Or somebody's said "Don't tell the Limeys".'

Salis raised his eyebrows and pushed his glasses back up to the bridge of his nose.

'I guess what you just said is an example of British humour.'

'No, it's not, Jake. I mean it and I'm not guessing.'

Salis stood up, and Farrow said, 'Don't go Jake because I've spoken to Sir John unofficially and if we don't get to the bottom of this it means that all co-operation between CIA and SIS London will finish as of today.'

Salis looked at Anders, whose face was impassive, and

then back at Farrow. 'You mean you'd break off our relationship because we don't break a code quickly enough. Is that it?'

Farrow shook his head slowly. 'No Jake, not at all. If it happened, we should be breaking off our co-operation because when we asked NSA for code-breaking help through the CIA they broke the code, or maybe already had it broken, and for their own good reasons didn't want us to have it.'

As Salis opened his mouth to speak, Farrow held his hand up. 'Your turn next Jake. Now NSA would only hold up a code on the instructions of CIA and that means that either they don't keep you in the picture or you're part of the fun and games. Right now we're in the middle of a set-to with the Poles and the Soviets. We monitor their signals traffic but we haven't got the code. You have but you don't pass it on. Either way Jake, it makes a nonsense of our co-operation. If they haven't told you then they don't trust the relationship; if they have told you then the relationship isn't worth a damn.'

Farrow leaned back in his chair and looked straight at Salis with no pretence of amiability. Salis was silent for a few moments and then he spoke quietly. 'First of all let me say that if this is true then I have not been kept in the picture, and that being so, I should raise a lot of hell. Second, I'd like to ask if you have proof of what you have just said.'

Farrow nodded, and didn't look one whit appeased. 'Yesterday we passed a piece of information to the Russians. It wasn't true. I made it up, and I arranged for Hallet to pass it to Venturi, the GRU man who's holed up in the Polish embassy. Nobody, not even Tad Anders here knows what I've done. Just me, Hallet and Venturi. So what happens? There's a heap of radio traffic in the code that we haven't broken. Then their survey ship *Pyotr Illyich* makes top speed to the spot I indicated. O.K. that's what you'd expect. But I did this for one reason only. I no longer believed you hadn't broken the code and I no longer believed we had CIA co-operation. So if I'm right your boys in Grosvenor Square will monitor the Polish embassy transmissions. They'll pass them back to NSA at Fort

George Meade who'll decode it, they'll see the stuff we've given the GRU man and they'll be off to the scene themselves.'

Farrow leaned forward and slapped a large hand on the table. 'Which is exactly what they have done. The nuclear sub you have on station to the east of the Orkneys left her station unguarded for the first time in two years and came thrashing down the North Sea. And right now she's sitting there just below the surface having a real bad time, watching the *Pyotr Illyich* send down divers and magnets and bathyscaphes and God knows what, looking for something that isn't there and never has been.'

Salis said, 'You're quite sure of this Colonel Farrow.'

Anders chipped in. 'Jake this is important to us and it's important to you.' He pushed across two pieces of paper. 'There's the Admiralty Intelligence sitrep covering your sub – it's a "P" class job. There's the time schedule of the transmissions from the Polish embassy.'

Salis looked at them and studied them carefully then pushed them back over the table to Anders and sighed. 'This isn't going to be easy. If we had indicated that we were not interested in your problems covering Venturi and Hallet it would have been O.K. for us not to get involved in the code problem. Agreed?' Neither Farrow nor Anders replied but they looked as if they were willing to listen, and Salis went on. 'It has always been accepted that either one of us could opt out of any operation, or never get involved so ...'

Farrow interrupted sharply, 'Jake, neither applies – you didn't opt out, you pretended to come in, your people took what was going and held back vital information.'

Salis looked at both of them and rubbing the side of his jaw said, 'O.K. what is it you people want? An apology from me, from Langley, the code or what? I'm going to be mighty angry, but nobody back in the States is going to worry too much about that. They'll want to put it right, of that I'm sure, and I guess you guys will have a deal in mind.'

'It's simple. We want all the decoded material covering this affair. Say from 24 July this year.'

'O.K. That sounds fair. Any significance in that date – 24 July?'

'Yes.'

Salis looked as if he were waiting for further explanation. He didn't get it, and he shrugged and moved to the door. 'I'll be back on to you shortly. I'm sure they'll have me on my knees to you. See you.'

It was two hours later when Salis phoned back to Farrow.

'Ed I've spoken to headquarters and I'm afraid I've got bad news. It's no dice, they won't agree. I understand the word came from on high.'

'You mean the President?'

'I mean the White House. I don't know precisely who.'

There was a long silence at both ends. Farrow hadn't expected this reaction. Either the Americans were being bloody-minded, which happened from time to time, or the Russians had been transmitting material that Washington valued and didn't want the British to see. His mind was racing through the loose ends of the affair and he reckoned that he had one trump card to play.

'I think Jake, that we'll have to treat this as the end of our co-operation. And if the White House has been told of this possibility and still fails to co-operate, I'm sure they'll accept the position.'

'I gather they do accept it colonel. I've been told to pack my bags and leave today.'

Farrow chose his words carefully. 'And what about the other fellow Jake?' He could sense the surprise at the other end. 'What other fellow?'

'The other CIA man. The one at the Hilton pretending he's on a Senate scientific mission. Red Murphy.'

There was a long silence at the other end until Salis said, 'Colonel I think we'd better meet together somewhere and discuss this further. Where can we meet?'

'Let's make it the foyer of the Hilton.'

'When?'

'Can you make it in half an hour?'

'I'll make it.'

*   *   *

129

They both ordered whisky and they sat in the dim light of the bar.

Salis was the first to broach the subject.

'I'd like to say first of all that I did *not* know about the code or about Murphy until you told me and I called my HQ today. You know as well as I do that there always will be areas where our interests don't coincide, where both governments have different objectives. So far these areas have never created real problems. A little friction maybe but no real trouble. It seems that in this particular case, we happen to have been working on it a long time before your people showed any interest. When you came to us about the code they were surprised, and for perhaps wrong reasons it was decided not to co-operate, and in addition not make clear that we were not co-operating. I'm pretty sure that this was only because it would have shown up our own interest in Hallet.'

Farrow held up his glass. 'I can accept all that Jake but once it's got to this stage with the Poles and the Russians it's time that you told us.'

'Do you think we could do a deal as of now?'

'What have you got in mind?'

'We'll pool all we know with your outfit. With you.'

'Nothing kept back?'

'Nothing.'

Farrow looked questioningly at Salis. 'You got the authority for this?'

Salis nodded. 'Yes. I'll prove it if you want it proved. I'll prove good faith anyway.'

'O.K.'

Salis was watching Farrow's face. 'Hallet's blonde is ours and Red Murphy is her control.'

CHAPTER XXI

Farrow was up at seven the next morning. The mist on the Thames was almost fog and for once the river seemed still and silent. After shaving he decided he'd have a small treat and walk to Sloane Square, and breakfast in style at the Royal Court Hotel. The fog was lifting as he walked up Lower Sloane Street and he stopped for the morning papers picking up *The Times*, the *Daily Mail* and a copy of the previous day's *Die Welt*. Across the square itself the pigeons clustered, necks huddled from the cold, no strutting or cooing for the benefit of early morning road sweepers.

Inside the Royal Court Hotel it was warm and cosy and he was made welcome, not because they knew him, but because they were Swiss and knew what hotels should be like.

So it was good oatmeal porridge, a well smoked steak of Fynnan haddock topped with Normandy butter and a poached egg. Then toast and Tiptree marmalade, coffee and a look at the papers.

And bang on the front page of the *Daily Mail* was the picture of the girl. It had been decently cut short but all too plain was the body arched in pain so that it seemed indecent to feel desire for the magnificent breasts upthrust to ease her tortured arm. The face of the man behind her was blown up alongside the picture and beside it was the identity photograph on the Soviet embassy's application for a diplomatic visa for entry to the United Kingdom. The details of the girl's incarceration were given with cross reference to the Ambassador's lying statements. There was a long editorial on the Russians' constant abuse of diplomatic privilege, and the brutality of the KGB, even in foreign countries.

Farrow looked at his watch, paid his bill and walked slowly back to the boat. The red light was winking on his phone and when he phoned through to central messages there was a note to phone Jake Salis.

'It's Ed Farrow, Jake, I think you want to speak to me.'

'Yes Ed, I've had a summary of decoded traffic from the Poles and the Russians. They were tipped off at ten-thirty yesterday evening about the picture of the girl in today's papers. Some stooge in one of the printers' unions phoned them. They tried to agitate for a walk-out but the men wouldn't play. The chat went on through the night and about an hour ago the Polish embassy got instructions to burn codebooks and so on to be ready for withdrawal tonight.'

'Who are they withdrawing, did they cover that?'

'The whole lot Ed. The Ambassador and all his staff except four or five tough guys who are going to stay behind with the girl. They'll use her as a hostage and fight it out. They want publicity for the British being rough, then they can play rough with your people in Warsaw and Moscow. They're going to leave their affairs in the hands of the Czech embassy. They're hoping you'll use troops so that they've got pictures and film for the UN and home consumption.'

'Thanks Jake, this'll help us a lot. We're going to be treading around in a minefield here and at least we know where some of the mines are. I'll keep you posted.'

The police doubled the barriers at both ends of Weymouth Street and at ten o'clock the Polish Ambassador phoned the Foreign Office that the whole of his staff would be leaving at mid-day and that he was unable, because of the conditions, to attend the usual courtesies of departure at the Foreign Office. The Foreign Secretary had taken the call personally and when Borowski announced that this was a withdrawal on the orders of Warsaw, as both a formal and physical ending of diplomatic relations, the Foreign Secretary had said, 'I shall send one of my officials down to you, your Excellency, and perhaps you will put this statement in writing. Am I to understand that all your staff will be leaving and that the embassy building will be empty?'

132

'We shall be leaving a small caretaker staff of about half a dozen.'

'And the girl?'

'She will be staying with the skeleton staff.

A police escort had been provided for the staff and their luggage and the long convoy of cars and trucks had wound its way through the East End down to the docks at Tilbury where the party had been awaited by the Polish ship *Stefan Batory*.

The mid-afternoon editions of the evening papers carried pictures and a full report on page one, and the radio news-bulletins at mid-day had given half the programme to the unprecedented action of the Poles.

The police moved the barriers in Weymouth Street nearer to the embassy building to cause the minimum of public inconvenience, and shortly after this small operation had been completed a man came out of the building and, looking up and down the street, walked over to the group of police officers. He stood talking to them for some minutes and then walked back to the embassy and the doors were closed. The Chief Inspector who had listened to the man then gave instructions for men to be sent to cover the back of the building. He also gave instructions for the occupants of all the adjoining buildings to be telephoned to evacuate them. Not in panic but with none of the high spirits that civilians sometimes get on the periphery of danger. Finally he radioed his headquarters and gave them the news that the group in the embassy wanted Hallet brought to them otherwise the girl would be shot.

The Home Secretary called an emergency meeting of those concerned with the Hallet affair. They already had the basic news before they arrived so there was little time spent on the preliminaries.

Nearly half an hour was given over to discussing whether the police or the army would have the responsibility for the operation. It was finally decided that the police would be in charge since, if the army took over, the public might look for quick and bloody action, whereas the police image would not be damaged by a display of patience and in-activity.

133

As events were likely to cover a mixture of violence, weapon fire, negotiation, diplomatic embroilment and warding off the press, it was decided that the total operation would remain in the hands of SIS in the shape of Ed Farrow assisted by Tad Anders.

Large-scale plans of the building and the surrounding area had been mounted on hardboard and a Parachute Regiment major described the current army practice for 'winkling out' in these sort of conditions. When he had finished an SIS officer who had had direct experience of Middle East terrorist activities, gave the group the benefit of his experiences in negotiating with terrorists. It included an authentic psychoanalysis of the terrorist mind and their aberrant reactions to what appeared to be normal counter-measures.

The Home Secretary turned to Farrow and taking off his glasses and cleaning them with a tissue said, without looking at him directly, 'So now Colonel Farrow, I don't expect details but I'd like to hear your intentions – if you're ready to talk that is.'

'Well sir, I've no intention of bargaining with these people at all. We've all seen what has gone on with the Arab terrorists. Threats, offers, counter-deals and the rest while the world's press and broadcasters report every raised eyebrow.

'These people want Hallet and they are not going to get him, that is point one. The second is that I don't intend indulging in a long drawn-out charade. I intend clearing the whole area around the embassy and withdrawing the police at least one hundred yards from the building. The telephones will be disconnected. Water, gas and electricity will be cut off, and if they have a transmitter it will be jammed as soon as we detect the frequency.'

The Commissioner of Police asked, 'How do you propose communicating with these people colonel?'

'There won't *be* any communication Commissioner, that's what's always wrong with these situations. They will have no communication whatsoever. Not with us, the press, not by telephone, letter, shouting, or radio. They will be in a vacuum. They can issue no threats because no one can hear them. If one of them walks out he'll get a warning

134

shot at his legs and if he still comes on he'll be fired at with intent to kill.'

The Home Secretary looked non-committal. 'And how does it all finish colonel? What if they want to call it a day?'

'Then they use the universal surrender sign sir, they hang out a white flag.'

A Permanent Secretary at the FO spoke. 'I wonder if the public won't find it distasteful that a girl is put in such jeopardy.'

'Then we'll tell the press and radio people the facts – that she's been working for the CIA – as an agent – without our knowledge.'

The Permanent Secretary nodded. 'What about the Danish and American reaction?'

Farrow half-smiled. 'We won't be there and I suspect that their public reaction will be against the people who recruited the girl and used her. They got her in this mess not us. I'd be willing to swop her for Red Murphy if he wants to volunteer – no I won't. I won't negotiate, period. These people are going to be in limbo.'

'Well gentlemen,' said the Home Secretary, 'has anyone any fundamental objection to Colonel Farrow's approach?' He looked around the table but his glance didn't linger. 'It's original anyway.' He nodded, stood up, and the meeting broke up.

One of the Poles was speaking to the telephone operator at the *Daily Express* when the line went dead, and gas and electricity supplies were cut off shortly afterwards. It was found to be impossible to cut off water supplies without affecting a hospital in the area.

Farrow checked over the list of monitored phone calls from the embassy after their call to the Foreign Office. There had been three calls to Hallet and Farrow dialled the number at the Ebury Street flat. There was no answer and when two men from Special Branch let themselves in about an hour later, the flat showed signs of hurriedly packed bags and a hasty departure. A general call was put out for Hallet to be brought in as soon as possible.

A quick check of the report by MI5 on the loading of

the MV *Batory* showed that Sergei Venturi was among the passengers. His name appeared on the passenger list as Third Secretary and both MI5 men had positively identified him.

During the afternoon various faces had been observed at the windows of the embassy. They had been photographed with infra-red film. It was processed and by mid-evening two of the four faces had been identified by Anders as thugs from the Z-11 training school.

Late afternoon saw the arrival of several batteries of Mole-Richardson lights. Their individual cables snaked back to a junction box in Portland Place where a thick cable took the combined load down the road to Broadcasting House. Temporary ramps for vehicles had been placed each side of the heavy cable.

There had been no movement at all during the evening, and at ten o'clock the street was still and deserted. Farrow had access through adjoining buildings to the observation team in the house opposite the embassy. He had given them routine instructions and was about to leave when Anders called on the radio net.

'Ed, the helicopter has taken off from the *Pyotr Illyich* and it's headed off on a course that should fetch up with the *Stefan Batory*. I've got a feeling that we haven't finished with Venturi.'

'Surely the *Batory* couldn't take a helicopter. It would thrash down all the stays.'

'I don't think they'll try that. The sea's quite calm. The forecast is force two to three, and I reckon they'll lower a net for Venturi and maybe they'll fuel as well.'

'Keep me in touch Tad, I'm busy right now.'

One of the observation party was signalling to him urgently and he moved over to the telescope. The door at the embassy was slightly open and somebody was standing just inside. Farrow pressed his microphone button and slid the switch to match the observation network which included the snipers. Then he spoke. 'Calling all marksmen. It looks as if one of the men may move out. I want marksmen seven and three to be responsible. If he does move out I want a warning shot from each of you as he gets to the bottom step. If he takes four paces in any for-

136

ward direction after that, without raising a flag of truce, you will both shoot him. Understood?'

He heard the crackle of agreement and switched off the microphone and waited. Nearly ten minutes passed and it had started to rain. There were no lights in any of the buildings and nobody in the street. In the distance the buildings were silhouetted by the lights of Oxford Street and Regent Street. It was like London in the blackout again but the atmosphere was different, the waiting and the silence were not companionable, they bred loneliness. The lamps blazed across the embassy building and were reflected in the wet surface of the road. From time to time a lamp was switched off to give the filament time to cool and the brilliant light would go out and then haunt the watchers' eyes till another was switched on. Then Farrow saw the man in the doorway move. He walked slowly forward and on the top step he looked backwards and spoke to somebody behind the heavy door. He laughed, and then looking up and down the street, he walked slowly down the steps standing on one for a moment. And as his foot touched the bottom step two shots rang out not quite together. Both splintered the stone step near where the man stood. He was looking to see where the shots came from but he was looking from bright light into the cavernous darkness behind the floodlights. He turned and had a shouted conversation with whoever was inside the embassy and then he rocked on his heels, gently and at ease. His hands in his trouser pockets and his jacket collar turned up against the slight rain. Then, with a faintly defiant smile, he stepped down from the last step to the roadway. His left foot was lifting to take the fourth step when the first shot hit him and snatched him round. The second hammered his head and punched it forward. His knees gave and he fell to the ground with his arms outstretched as if he felt he was falling into space.

He lay where he had fallen, without moving, and as Farrow looked through the powerful telescope he could see blood pumping from a hole behind the man's right ear. The radio crackled in Farrow's hand and he acknowledged the call sign. 'Shall we go and collect him chief?'

'No, just leave him there.' Then he switched off.

137

He could sense the disbelief and the dislike without hearing the words.

He was sure that the men in the embassy would soon be in a bad state. They'd planned to bargain and counterbargain for Hallet. They were built for action not for waiting, and he wanted to make them feel that all they had been told by Venturi, about how the situation would develop, had been wrong.

The man lying dead in the road wasn't part of the Venturi plan and the fact that he'd been left lying there was an indication of what was to come. Venturi's plan was beginning to look pointless. There was no one to threaten, no one to bargain with. If they killed the girl it would make no difference, the others wouldn't know and if they did it just made their own deaths more certain. The percentages were all wrong. They decided to wait for Venturi's transmission before they acted.

Farrow went back to the Joint Intelligence Bureau to meet Anders and Salis. Anders reported that Venturi had been hoisted from the *Batory* and taken to the *Pyotr Illyich*. Farrow asked Salis for the back material from monitoring the Polish transmissions. He looked quickly through for certain dates and checking with one of his own files he said, 'Right Jake. Let's just sort this out. You people knew about the codeword "Omega Minus" from the girl. She knew because she had been with Hallet in his office when he put up the codeword on his visual display unit. *We* didn't know this until Hallet told me a couple of days ago. Now in this signals traffic from Moscow control, they were referring to "Omega Minus" a few days after the girl told CIA. So who did they get it from? Not from us – we didn't know. Not from the girl – she was working for you. Not from Hallet, he had no contact till Venturi went to the cottage. So who told them?'

Salis looked back at Farrow. 'Who've you got in mind?'

'Jake you've got a leak back at CIA Langley.'

'I'll get on to them right now and I'll request permission not to transmit my current reports until this operation is over.'

'You might point out to them that if we had been cooperating this wouldn't have happened.'

138

'I won't Ed. They'll grasp the point without me saying so, and I'm not all that popular at the moment.'

When Salis had gone Anders pushed across a typewritten report. It read: FARROW JOIN TINT BUREAU STOP HALLET OBSERVED NEWCASTLE STATION EX INTER-CITY OUT OF LONDON STOP UNDER OBSERVATION QUERY ARREST STOP AWAIT INSTRUCTIONS MATHEWS MESSAGE ENDS.

Farrow looked up. 'Thank Christ somebody's using his head. Can you do this for me Tad, ask him to keep Hallet under observation and fix him up with one of the small transceivers? Put an operator on it full-time at this end, and get Mathews to keep in continuous touch. He's got to report at least every five minutes. Fly two men up to make a team with him.'

It was an hour later when Farrow phoned through for a continuous radio and radar check on the *Pyotr Illyich*. But he was too late.

CHAPTER XXII

Venturi had checked the charts of the coast above Tyne-mouth again and again, and he'd always come back to the deep bay just north of Bamburgh. Seahouses, Beadnell and Craster would give them better shelter but there were houses and farmsteads near and they would almost certainly be observed. Budie Bay went almost a mile and a half inland and the bottom was soft sand. There would be easy beaching for the boats and they were unlikely to be seen.

So the *Pyotr Illyich* had threaded her way well clear of the Farnes and had anchored 10 miles east of Holy Island. The two ship's boats had been lowered from their davits and Venturi and his small force had taken a bearing on Guile Point and then edged down the coast along the Ross Back Sands. It was half an hour short of dawn when they edged into Budie Bay and back up the finger of sheltering land. The boats were pulled up clear of the high water mark, the radios were checked and Venturi supervised the erection of the camouflage nets that were to shelter the crews.

The man from Newcastle had been waiting with the van at the junction of the road to Belford. He took Venturi's kit and put it in the back. As he started the engine he said, 'I've found a place for us to use, comrade. It's been empty for a year, nobody goes there and it's not too far away from here.' As they moved off southwards the massive rock-like fortress of Bamburgh Castle was just visible in the early morning light.

They kept to the coast road and at Seahouses the light was good enough to see the Farnes, and Venturi checked his compass with a bearing on the Longstone Lighthouse. His chart showed an 8 degrees 41 minutes west magnetic variation and he made the calculation and drew the bearing. The pencilled line ran directly through the lighthouse on the western outcrop of Longstone. He did the same check on the lighthouse on Farne itself and then radioed his position to the ship.

The small town of Seahouses was closed and empty as they went through. The van followed the sharp right-hand bend at the approach to Beadnell and straight on to the Swinhoe junction, then down the twisting, narrow road to Embleton. At the edge of Longhoughton they turned left and took the coast road through Boulmer village. Half an hour later they had slowly circled the perimeter of RAF Boulmer. There was nothing changed so far as Venturi could see.

The van went back up the road to Embleton and on for another two miles, then the driver slowed down at a sharp right turn and then an S-bend. Through the trees Venturi could see the house – it was long, with the eastern end a collection of barns and cottages. On the gates the stone pillars were carved with clover leaves and the inscription 'Newton Hall'. The rising sun put flashes on the big windows and set fire to the flaming autumn colours of Virginia creeper that covered the whole of the front. They drove on to a third set of gates and the driver eased the van into the shelter of a large barn. Venturi checked his stop-watch and the Englishman stepped down from the cab and closed the double gates in the yard.

The Hall was for sale and had not been occupied for almost a year. A woman from the village came every second week to dust and switch on the central heating for an hour or so. She was not due for another ten days. The lock on the back door needed a squirt of oil and then it turned and snapped back and Venturi walked in.

There was an old-fashioned kitchen with hooks for hanging meat carcasses from the ceiling. Two pantries, a scullery, and then a bathroom. There were three large rooms on the ground floor and a huge hall that gave on to wide stairs. Upstairs there was a maze of rooms and two bathrooms.

Farrow had slept for four hours and then he'd been awakened to be told of the situation in Northumberland. Hallet had hired a car at Newcastle and driven up the A1 to Alnwick. He had driven quite slowly as if he were in no hurry. At Alnwick he'd taken a room at the White Swan hotel. He had walked to the bookshop in Bondgate Without and had bought several paperbacks and a local ordnance survey map before walking back to the hotel where he had had dinner served in his room.

The *Pyotr Illyich* had maintained radio silence and Farrow was not aware of the landing of the two boats and their crews. But he guessed that some sort of rendezvous had been made between Hallet and Venturi, or somebody representing Venturi.

He phoned Anders and they met at the Battersea heliport. They touched down an hour later at Alnmouth.

CHAPTER XXIII

Hallet had been demented with worry about the girl and the 'lift' that he had got from his talk with Farrow had melted away when he saw that the photograph had appeared in the newspapers.

He had phoned Venturi from a call box and begged him to release the girl. At the first call Venturi had been friendly but had said that there was no way to release the girl. When Hallet had continued to plead with him he had suggested he phoned again in an hour's time. At the second call Hallet had gone from pleading to bluster and, as he was speaking, he heard the girl's screams at the other end. They were high pitched and terrible and he heard her call his name and then she was screaming in agony and the phone had gone dead. He had dialled again immediately, his fingers hardly able to control the dial. Venturi had told him what he had to do to obtain the girl's release. He'd carried out his instructions dutifully and now awaited the telephone call that should open the door for the girl.

He hated being on his own but he was afraid of walking in the town in case he were recognized. So he sat in the rather gloomy room waiting for the telephone call. He looked again at the paperbacks on the bed; there was that lifeboat of the reading man, Gibbon's *Decline and Fall*, bought once again and probably once more to be abandoned; there was the final volume of C. P. Snow's great saga and he didn't need to look to recall what was the third. He reached out for it and turned once again to the poem. The title stood out. The print seemed over-large where it said – 'To Aurora' – and he read on. 'O, if thy pride did not our joys control —', and he closed the book because he couldn't bear to read more. It seemed a hundred years ago. The self-assured, confident happiness seemed as far away as childhood. When the girl had first been kidnapped he had been shocked by his continued desire for her, he had had visions of the girl and her breasts and open legs and over-riding his shame he had thought it a waste that he would not be having her that night. And now he dare not think of her in terms of sex any more. The photograph of the two men with the girl had been the torture it was meant to be. What else had they done to her? Surely it could not have been just anger or indifference – there must have been lust. What else did they do to her? His mind sprang away from it as like poles spring away, and yet it never really left him. How would they be when it was all over? Would the girl ever again be looking with those bright, shining eyes, alight with healthy youth and excitement as she opened her long shapely legs to excite him? He shook his head like a dog plunging out of the sea, and threw the book across the room.

There was no telephone call that night and Hallet slept fitfully as if he were fevered. It was ten o'clock the next morning before the call came. It was not Venturi, it was a man with a Tyneside accent and the pinched Geordie vowels sounded like Swedish.

He had paid his bill and driven back to the column with the rampant Percy lion at the approach to Alnwick, and there he'd turned left. Past the long view of the castle and over the River Aln and the A1. Past the sign that pointed right, to Boulmer. The gates of the Hall were open and a man standing there signalled him to drive the car alongside the van in the barn. Then he was taken to Venturi.

Mathews had followed Hallet until he saw him turn into Newton Hall and he had driven on a quarter of a mile to the next phone box. Inside he had reported the situation by radio and had waited while he was linked in to Farrow at Alnmouth.

'Have you any information on the house?'

'No sir, apart from my description and its location.'

'Is it possible to carry out observation of the house without being seen?'

'I'm doubtful sir.'

'Right. Keep a watch on the house from as far as you can get and still see it. You say there are three double gates?'

'Yes that's right sir.'

'They all lead on to the road?'

'Yes.'

'Just keep them under observation and keep reporting. When's your relief due?'

'Not for three hours.'

'Fine, off you go.'

Anders had already contacted the county police HQ at Morpeth. It seemed that Newton Hall was owned by an elderly couple now living in Bermuda. Had been vacant for a year and was for sale. Then the report had come through from London of a message from Jake Salis. He had had a message from the NSA at Fort George Meade, via the CIA's HQ at Langley. It gave the movements of the *Pyotr Illyich* in her wanderings near the Farnes and Holy Island. It also informed them of the launching of two small boats, approximately 30-footers, which had left the spy-boat during the night. The message commented that radio silence had been maintained for four hours prior to the boats leaving.

Mathews' reports were reports of 'nothing to observe' until mid-morning and then a gate in the high wall of the walled garden had opened and a man dressed in slightly naval gear had walked out and stood looking across the fields towards Beadnell Bay. After lighting a cigarette he'd walked round the three visible sides of the garden wall and then back into the garden. He'd had a sub-machine gun slung over his shoulder. It seemed to confirm that Venturi was staked out at Newton Hall.

Signals Security had reported radio traffic from the vicinity of the house. Tapes had been made and played back to Farrow by telephone. They were voices, not Morse, they were in Russian and the speaker was Venturi.

Newton Hall was built on a slight mound which gave it the air of a moated castle, for the ground fell away in every direction. To the west was a small stream that divided the house from some of its adjoining fields. A large walled garden covered a quarter of an acre to the north and on its eastern side the house and out-buildings ran to the dry stone wall that flanked the road to Beadnell. The house itself faced south and looked on to rolling lawns that were

145

encircled by a wide, gravel drive. A spread of elms and beeches that followed the driveway gave privacy to the house without restricting the outward view. For as it stood on its small plateau most of the front windows gave sight of the deserted beaches and sand dunes.

Farrow was trying to work out in his mind what Venturi would do and whichever way he assessed the situation it was clear that Venturi would fight it out. He was too much of a professional not to have radioed any hard information that he had obtained from Hallet and this had not happened. The only radio traffic out of Newton Hall since Hallet's call there, had been 'in clear', and only straight-forward situation reports.

Another radio message came through from London that the men at the Polish embassy had surrendered. They had walked out with the girl, carrying a white flag. It seemed that the men were being returned immediately to Warsaw. It was part of a deal with the Poles. The Polish embassy would remain empty for two months and no action would be taken against the British embassy in Warsaw in exchange for the men. The girl had been in bad shape physically and mentally, and had been handed over to the United States embassy who had flown her to Texas in a USAAF plane.

The house was still and their footsteps echoed as they walked through the kitchen, down a short corridor, across a large hall to a heavy door that seemed to be locked. The man knocked on the door and waited. A few moments later a key turned in the lock and the door was opened by Venturi.

Inside, the room was sparsely furnished. There was a large round table, two armchairs, a chest of drawers and a few chairs set at the table. The autumn sun was slanting through the side window across the round table. It lit a small radio with a filament aerial trailing up to the high ceiling and held there with a patch of Sellotape. There was coal in the old-fashioned fireplace but no fire, and everywhere there was the smell of dust and neglect.

Venturi waved Hallet to one of the upright chairs and turned back to the charts and maps that he was studying on the table. He looked drawn and tired but with a sharp alertness that showed that although he was working under extreme pressure he was working with confidence. Experience and training had been for precisely these situations when professionalism could turn apparent disaster into success. Finally Venturi threw down his pencil, looked at Hallet and stood up.

'Well Hallet, I haven't time for discussion so we must come quickly to the facts. Take everything from your pockets.'

Slowly Hallet placed the contents of his pockets on the table. Venturi pushed the wallet and the keys to one side, sorted through the other items and then searched Hallet skilfully and thoroughly. Then he went through every item in Hallet's wallet. Since Moscow had taken over the operation he had seen his careful planning disintegrate under the orders of men whose determination was matched by their ignorance of operating in the outside world. Maybe they knew something he didn't know but from the moment he'd been ordered to kidnap the girl he had known that the planners of the KGB and the GRU had been swept aside. The last time that had happened had been over the Cuban missile sites and from the moment the politicians took over it had been a downward slide to disaster and inevitable nuclear war or submission. If the politicians had taken over 'Omega Minus' then it must be big but he knew all too well that only Hallet mattered.

Venturi had been informed by Moscow that there were possible clues to Hallet's discovery stashed away in coded information in the computer at Hallet's office. That was virtually inaccessible and similar information on GRU computers would be programmed for instant erasure if access was attempted without adhering to a complex formula. Hallet would have certainly taken similar precautions. But it was a long-term possibility that Venturi valued in case all else failed. Hallet's keys would be insurance for the future. Best of all would have been the removal of Hallet to Moscow and that was why Venturi had risked returning after his easy departure with the Polish embassy staff. And finally, and almost as valuable, would be the 'Omega Minus' device itself. There was a specialist labora-

147

tory in a basement of the Serp i Molot steel works on the outskirts of Moscow that would be able to analyse and synthesize the operation and function from the device itself.

Venturi looked back at Hallet and studied his face. The eyes were red-rimmed with sleeplessness and there was a tic at the side of his mouth that he couldn't control and he was breathing through his mouth. It angered Venturi that so much should depend on a man like this. He guessed he had no more than an hour to get what he wanted. He held up the bunch of keys in front of Hallet.

'Touch each one Hallet and tell me what it's for.'

Hallet hesitated and then as Venturi spread the keys on his palm Hallet pointed with his forefinger. 'That's the ignition key of the car – the Lamborghini, and that's the car door key. This is the front door key at the cottage and this is for the flat in Ebury Street.' He stopped and looked at Venturi. He went on, 'That's a special key for my office.' Venturi looked at him without blinking, 'And these?'

'That's an AA key, that's my bank deposit box key and...', he hesitated for a moment, '...and that's an access key to the computer.'

Venturi lifted the big office key. 'What's special about it?'

Hallet said quickly, 'What arrangements are you going to make about the girl?'

Venturi felt a flash of anger at the weak man's attempt at bargaining but he kept his anger under control. 'Hallet you'd better understand right now that we're not playing games any more. If you co-operate the girl will stay alive. If you don't she'll be killed.'

Hallet hadn't seen the danger signs and he said, 'How do I know you haven't killed her already, you said ...'

Venturi felt almost faint with anger as he reached out for Hallet. He had both hands round his throat and then with obvious willpower he released him. His voice was trembling with anger as he spoke and Hallet was conscious that the man's teeth were bared like an animal's as the words came tumbling out. 'I've warned you Hallet. You'll tell me what I want to know or I'll kill you now and before you go you can hear me give my men in Weymouth

148

Street a free hand with the girl. She'll die then, I assure you, but they'll have her till she's dead. Don't think that's the end of it – there's still your daughters at the school in Kent.'

He smashed his fist on the table. 'For the last time Hallet, it's not a bloody game.'

Hallet was trembling as he looked at Venturi. He looked far removed from the man who had sat in the cottage at Goudhurst in an old dressing-gown, talking quietly and calmly about Hallet helping his country. He took a deep breath. 'It works an electronic lock. There's a white dot on the key stem, you line it up with a similar white dot on the key slot on the door and you turn it the wrong way to open the door – anti-clockwise that is. Any other way and it sets off the alarms.'

'Where is your "Omega Minus" device?'

'It's at RAF Boulmer.'

'Where exactly?'

'In the Marconi hut where I worked.'

'Go on.'

'There's a row of shelves on one wall and it's on the top shelf. There are a number of old spare radio parts containers and one of them is marked with white paint with an Omega in Greek.'

'How big is it?'

'About 25 centimetres cube.'

'Colour?'

'Standard services grey-blue originally, the outer case is rather rusty now.'

Venturi moved over to the table and sat down. He flicked a switch on the radio and a small red diode flickered and finally glowed as he released the tuning knob. Then he was giving a call sign in Russian, but there was no response. He switched channels and then he could hear the heavy beat of powerful jamming. It was so loud he knew the transmitter must be within twenty miles. He guessed it was probably at RAF Boulmer. That meant his link to the *Pyotr Illyich* was cut. He changed channels again to contact the landing party at Budie Bay. He gave the call sign and then with a lot of static he heard them responding.

Then the other man with the sub-machine gun walked

in. He was obviously agitated and Venturi turned down the volume. 'What is it Henson?'

'There's a fellow in the phone box. Been there at least two hours. He's watching this place. Got a car in a turning up the lane to Newton Grange Farm. I've taken the distributor . . .' and he showed Venturi the brown plastic rotor arm.

'Is the van ready?'

'Aye guv'nor, we'd better be moving.'

Venturi had packed up the papers and the radio and they'd walked through the house and out to the barn. They had tied Hallet's hands behind his back and dumped him in the back of the small van. At Swinhoe crossroads they'd gone straight on, avoiding the main road. It was half an hour before they got to the junction at Belford. The driver turned the van down the main road and parked by the council notice declaring the bay a protected area for birds and other wild life. Venturi stepped out and Hallet saw that there was a gun pointing at him. It was a 9-mm. Makarov and Venturi's hand closed round it as if it had been specially moulded to fit his hand. It had.

Without the balance of his arms Hallet stumbled and Venturi caught him before he fell and then pointed to the white post and rail fence and told him to duck under it. The van drove off and there had been no good-byes as Venturi carried the radio and a canvas bag under the rail and down a steep bank. There was a dry wall curving up over the hill and the fold of the hill was covered in gorse bushes almost to the edge of the bay. The tide was out and the sun shone across the mud flats. Then suddenly Venturi pulled him to the ground in the overhang of one of the giant gorses. A few moments later Hallet saw a flash of light from the direction of the sea, then he could hear the clatter of a helicopter and as they watched, a helicopter came from the sea across the bay. The RAF roundels looked fresh and clean in the clear light and it came lower as it reached the inner limit of the bay where they were lying, and then turned slowly and started back seawards.

It was only just over 2 miles to the landing party and Venturi knew that if he could get Hallet to the boats they would stand a good chance of getting to the *Pyotr Illyich.*

Venturi shoved the pistol against Hallet's chest and spoke quietly. 'You will run along with me comrade and when I drop you will drop. You make one mistake and I'll finish you. Understand?'

They had done nearly a mile, stopping and sheltering in the big gorse bushes as the helicopter criss-crossed the bay area, but then the crew must have spotted them. It made its turn and headed back on the southern leg of its search pattern but after a couple of hundred yards it had just hung there, and then, tilting on its side, had turned back and slowly moved down lower and lower till it was clattering overhead about 80 feet above them. Someone was signalling with an Aldis lamp to the south-east and Venturi stood up and looked towards the distant road. A jeep was slowing and then it stopped and three men got out and started in their direction. An army sergeant was being lowered from the helicopter. He was experienced because he had one boot perfectly placed in the loop and he stood off from the rope holding it with one hand with ease and confidence. He had a ·38 Smith & Wesson army standard issue revolver in his hand. Hallet saw that he was grinning as he looked down at them and then suddenly there were two shots from beside him and the sergeant leaned backwards slowly, his hand loosed the rope and his beret fluttered down as his spread-eagled body seemed to hang for a moment as it turned head down and seconds later the ground shook beneath Hallet's feet.

Venturi rammed the gun in Hallet's back and for a few moments of pain he was cutting through the rope that bound Hallet's hands. As his hands came free Venturi said harshly 'Run with me to the sand bank over there'. And with another jolt from the gun Hallet was running. Venturi had abandoned the radio and his kit-bag and they were running and stumbling through the coarse tussocks of grass that edged the bay. Herring gulls, oystercatchers and terns rose from the sands and their shrieking wailing cries, as they wheeled out across the bay, grew faint and there was nothing but the sound of pebbles scattering under their feet and their gasping, heaving breath.

Behind them the helicopter had landed and Hallet could hear voices carried on the wind and suddenly they were running on wet sand and ahead of them he could see men. The landing party were pushing the boats to the shallow water and by the time they got to the boats the diesels were thumping regularly and the stem of each boat was held by only one man, the others were in the boats. Willing hands hauled up both of them as they splashed through water up to their waists. Hallet's heart was pounding from the running and he lay on the sole boards exhausted and sick with fear.

The men were laughing and shouting as Venturi waved to them to move off and the powerful engines soon had them in deeper water. There was no sign of the helicopter. Venturi had put the gun away. He obviously didn't need it any more. He looked tense with excitement and victory. Radio contact was made with the *Pyotr Illyich* and she set a direct course for the two boats. There were only ten miles of clear sea between them and the spy-boat's instruments gave no readings for any vessel nearer than 30 miles. The boats were out of territorial waters in twenty minutes, and it was a few minutes after that that they saw the helicopter.

CHAPTER XXIV

The sun filled the body of the helicopter with red autumn light and as they swung down towards the boats they could see their trailing wakes and the pilot calculated they must be doing 8 to 10 knots. As they came over the second time they could see the crews throwing cans and boxes of stores overboard to increase the speed. Farrow could see Venturi and then saw Hallet kneeling against a locker. Farrow waited till they had made a turn and gave the pilot his orders.

'I want to come in low enough for my loud-hailer to get to them, keep behind them if you can.' As they came in he saw puffs of smoke as they were fired at by the crews and then they were down. The starboard door was open and the loud-hailer crackled as he called out in Russian 'Venturi, Venturi, I want you to release Hallet. We'll put down a rope for him. If you co-operate we will take no further action. If you do not we will sink you.'

He moved the loud-hailer aside to look down at the trailing boat and he could see Venturi plainly and as he looked Venturi lifted his hand. The sign he made had the same meaning all over the world and he could see the flash of Venturi's grin. Then there was a clatter as some part of the fuselage was hit and as they made height a bullet shattered the Plexiglass window in the open door. They'd worked out that the helicopter wasn't armed.

They stood off clear of the boats while Farrow radioed his order to the two Mark 3 Harriers from Rothbury. They were already airborne and jilling around just south of Edinburgh when they got Farrow's order, and they had streaked their shuddering, ear-splitting course to the boats in 2·9 minutes. They came in low, one above the other, and only the lower aircraft opened fire. The two 30-mm. Aden cannon ripped off half their loads and then both aircraft were out of sight. The first boat had taken 70 of the 130 cannon that had been fired and it had disintegrated rather than sunk. One minute it had been there, then there had been a spray of wood and fire and in seconds the boat had disappeared. There were bodies floating just below the water and a man was swimming towards the second boat.

As they came in again there was no firing and the boat was not under power. It was rolling and making no way. Farrow called again on the loud-hailer, 'Venturi, Venturi, you are responsible for what has happened. Will you release Hallet now? Wave your hand if you will.'

He pulled aside the loud-hailer and watched Venturi. The man's anger was plain to see but Farrow knew that the crew would have him overboard if he did not comply with the order. Venturi knew it too. It would be mutiny but nobody would ever know. One of the crew lifted his arm to wave and Venturi was quicker.

Then Farrow knew he'd guessed right as he saw the sun glint on the pistol. Against the clatter of the rotors they could hear nothing else but he saw Hallet fall back and there was a curtain of blood coming up on his shirt. There was no doubt he was dead.

Venturi and Farrow were loners, and loners only survive if they count all the cards. Farrow had known, without actually thinking it, that one way or another Hallet's death was inevitable. The easy way out was to let him die with the rest of them when the fighter came back to attack the remaining boat. But even Hallet's death had to be twice covered. With Hallet dead they would all be back to square one. 'Omega Minus' was best buried at sea. If Venturi hadn't reacted as he expected then he'd have killed Hallet himself. But both sides of the Iron Curtain the basic training was much the same. He had known that Venturi would kill Hallet even if it made his own death certain.

As he watched he saw Venturi struggling with three men, and then Venturi was being pushed remorselessly backwards and his arms flew in the air instinctively. His body was snatched down into the swirl of the engine wake as the crew headed the boat towards the *Pyotr Illyich*. They were now only two miles apart but when the second Harrier flew back, the ship's boat had made little progress. She went down with all hands in just over a minute and

154

if the Harrier pilot had seen the white shirt on the upraised oar it had made no difference.

In one of the smaller offices deep in the main CIA building at Langley, two men sat on opposite sides of a large teak desk. Between them a medal lay in its plush presentation case. In the centre blue circle of enamel there were thirteen silver stars. It had more of the look of an order than a decoration, but it was, in fact, the Legion of Merit, and because it was for a foreigner, and a deserving foreigner, it was the second highest degree – a commander's.

The older man, he had white hair, had listened carefully but with obvious impatience. Then as the explanation finished he reached forward and straightened the medal so that it was squared up to his notepad.

'What is it Sam, she want more dough or what?'

The younger man shook his head.

'No Tom. I'm sure it's not that. You've seen the analyst's report. Says she's withdrawn but otherwise normal. And she doesn't like us.'

'She doesn't know us for God's sake.'

'I mean the CIA, Joe – the CIA in general.'

'She took the money?'

'Sure. I paid all her back pay and 10,000 bucks official bonus as promised way back.'

'What did she say when she refused the decoration?'

The younger man looked as if he shared the guilt as he said 'She just said, "Tell them to stuff it".'

'Those actual words?'

'Yes.'

'You told her it had been initiated in the White House?'

'Made no difference, Tom. She wasn't angry. She was cold as they come.'

The older man pushed back his chair and stood up. And the younger man looked up at him. 'I haven't finished yet, Tom.'

'About Miss Olsen?' And he sat down pulling the chair to the desk.

'She didn't want the operation.'

'Why not?'

'Says she wants to have the child.'

The older man was pulling off the cellophane from a thin cigar and without looking up he said,

'So?'

'She got to like Hallet. Wants his child.'

As the match flared, 'I thought she'd asked us to fix her up on a degree course at University of Texas?'

The younger man looked puzzled. 'Yes, she did. That's still on.'

'So. An unmarried mother and her baby will grace the campus at Austin.'

'Tom, she did everything the Agency asked of her and she's having a bad time right now.'

'What is it? Guilt about Hallet, or the baby or what?'

The younger man realized at that point that he was wasting his time.

'I'll keep an eye on her, Tom.'

The younger man had taken his white MG on to the Freeway down to Arlington and was at the Memorial bridge before he could put out of his mind the memory of the girl in the hospital bed. The long blonde hair had been spread over the fat pillows and the blue eyes had looked even bluer now that the tan had gone. She had listened as he talked, but she never responded, even though she spoke. Just that sexy Danish accent saying what she intended to do. As briefly as she could. As if words were a thousand dollars apiece. There had been a picture of her and Hallet feeding the pigeons in Trafalgar Square, and all the while the finger of her right hand touched a ring on her left hand, as if it were a talisman. He would read Hallet's file again. He wondered if a girl would ever feel like that about him.

Special Branch had opened up Hallet's office for Farrow and there they had found the key to the computer room. Farrow had bowed them out and then sat at Hallet's desk and read his notes on computers for the third time. The man from IBM had been patient and a good teacher, and Farrow was a thorough man. He started down in the basement. It took two hours moving computer discs and thousands of punched cards and tape to the incinerator, and Farrow had watched it all flame and burn till there was nothing left.

Back up in the office he checked every item in the big curved desk. There was very little apart from invitations to learned societies and circulars from publishers of scientific books. As he sat at Hallet's desk he looked around the room. It was a peaceful room and the noise of the traffic outside was barely audible. He walked to the long window and looked down on Sloane Square. The leaves from the plane trees were lining the gutters where the taxis stood on their rank, and the flower sellers had chrysanthemums and roses. It was a Sunday so Peter Jones was closed. He could just see the people in the King's Road. Everything seemed so normal and Farrow wondered what the strollers in Sloane Square would have said if they were told what went on in their name. Maybe like the people in Dzerzhinski Square they wouldn't believe it, and if they did they wouldn't give a damn.

At Hallet's flat there was a small pile of mail inside the door and Farrow sat at the coffee table to open and read it. It seemed a long time since he'd cleaned up this flat while talking to Hallet to get him to co-operate. In the end the man's basic weakness had pulled the plans of all of them down. Maybe there was a Gresham's Law of espionage.

There was a garage bill for work on the Lamborghini and a large envelope containing share certificates and receipts.

There was a letter from his wife:

Dear James,

I saw you on TV a few days ago and you looked very ill. I can understand how worried you must be at present.

I have told Bartlett to get on with the divorce immediately. I do not want to add to your troubles.

Have you seen the girls yet? I gather that Jill has a boyfriend (works at the school stables).

Please believe me when I say that I wish you much

157

happiness with your new lady. A lot of people round here ask nicely about you.

Love
Lolly.

And a note from his solicitors:

Dear Dr. Hallet,

We have been informed by Mrs. Hallet's solicitors that the hearing of the divorce petition is now set down for the 17th of next month.

We may require your attendance and will advise you in due course.

Yours faithfully,
James, Larter and Payne.

There was a small package addressed to the girl which Farrow opened carefully and slowly. It contained a diamond ring and a short note.

Dear Miss Olsen,

Your ring is enclosed and we think you will now find that it fits your finger more easily.

Always pleased to be at your service.

Yours faithfully,

Homet & James – the jewellers' jewellers.

There was a note on blue paper with the address of Benenden School:

Darling Daddy,

Mummy says you are coming to see us soon.

I have had ten riding lessons and Jill has had nine. There is a nice donkey in a field near here.

We went to Rye last week and I bought a book – 'The Daring Twins' – super. Do you remember when you took us rowing in Hyde Park and told us about the princess in the lake? We miss your stories daddy, so come and see us soon.

Lots and lots of love.
Patsy.

P.S. Did you enjoy New York?

Farrow burnt them all in the small grate.

THE PERENNIAL LIBRARY MYSTERY SERIES

Delano Ames

CORPSE DIPLOMATIQUE   P 637, $2.84
"Sprightly and intelligent."

—New York Herald Tribune Book Review

FOR OLD CRIME'S SAKE   P 629, $2.84

MURDER, MAESTRO, PLEASE   P 630, $2.84
"If there is a more engaging couple in modern fiction than Jane and
Dagobert Brown, we have not met them."   *—Scotsman*

SHE SHALL HAVE MURDER   P 638, $2.84
"Combines the merit of both the English and American schools in the
new mystery. It's as breezy as the best of the American ones, and has
the sophistication and wit of any top-notch Britisher."

—New York Herald Tribune Book Review

E. C. Bentley

TRENT'S LAST CASE   P 440, $2.50
"One of the three best detective stories ever written."

—Agatha Christie

TRENT'S OWN CASE   P 516, $2.25
"I won't waste time saying that the plot is sound and the detection
satisfying. Trent has not altered a scrap and reappears with all his old
humor and charm."   *—Dorothy L. Sayers*

Gavin Black

A DRAGON FOR CHRISTMAS   P 473, $1.95
"Potent excitement!"   *—New York Herald Tribune*

THE EYES AROUND ME   P 485, $1.95
"I stayed up until all hours last night reading *The Eyes Around Me,*
which is something I do not do very often, but I was so intrigued by the
ingeniousness of Mr. Black's plotting and the witty way in which he spins
his mystery. I can only say that I enjoyed the book enormously."

—F. van Wyck Mason

YOU WANT TO DIE, JOHNNY?   P 472, $1.95
"Gavin Black doesn't just develop a pressure plot in suspense, he adds
uninfected wit, character, charm, and sharp knowledge of the Far East
to make rereading as keen as the first race-through."   *—Book Week*

THOU SHELL OF DEATH　　　　　　　P 428, $1.95
"It has all the virtues of culture, intelligence and sensibility that the most exacting connoisseur could ask of detective fiction."
　　　　　　　　　　—*The Times* [London] *Literary Supplement*

THE WIDOW'S CRUISE　　　　　　　P 399, $2.25
"A stirring suspense. . . . The thrilling tale leaves nothing to be desired."
　　　　　　　　　　—*Springfield Republican*

THE WORM OF DEATH　　　　　　　P 400, $2.25
"It [The Worm of Death] is one of Blake's very best—and his best is better than almost anyone's."　　　　　　—Louis Untermeyer

John & Emery Bonett

A BANNER FOR PEGASUS　　　　　　　P 554, $2.40
"A gem! Beautifully plotted and set. . . . Not only is the murder adroit and deserved, and the detection competent, but the love story is charming."　　　　　　—Jacques Barzun and Wendell Hertig Taylor

DEAD LION　　　　　　　P 563, $2.40
"A clever plot, authentic background and interesting characters highly recommended this one."　　　　　　—*New Republic*

Christianna Brand

GREEN FOR DANGER　　　　　　　P 551, $2.50
"You have to reach for the greatest of Great Names (Christie, Carr, Queen . . .) to find Brand's rivals in the devious subtleties of the trade."
　　　　　　　　　　—Anthony Boucher

TOUR DE FORCE　　　　　　　P 572, $2.40
"Complete with traps for the over-ingenious, a double-reverse surprise ending and a key clue planted so fairly and obviously that you completely overlook it. If that's your idea of perfect entertainment, then seize at once upon *Tour de Force.*"　　　　—Anthony Boucher, *The New York Times*

James Byrom

OR BE HE DEAD　　　　　　　P 585, $2.84
"A very original tale . . . Well written and steadily entertaining."
　　　—Jacques Barzun & Wendell Hertig Taylor, *A Catalogue of Crime*

Henry Calvin

IT'S DIFFERENT ABROAD P 640, $2.84
"What is remarkable and delightful, Mr. Calvin imparts a flavor of satire to what he renovates and compels us to take straight."

—Jacques Barzun

Marjorie Carleton

VANISHED P 559, $2.40
"Exceptional . . . a minor triumph."
—Jacques Barzun and Wendell Hertig Taylor, *A Catalogue of Crime*

George Harmon Coxe

MURDER WITH PICTURES P 527, $2.25
"[Coxe] has hit the bull's-eye with his first shot."

—*The New York Times*

Edmund Crispin

BURIED FOR PLEASURE P 506, $2.50
"Absolute and unalloyed delight."

—Anthony Boucher, *The New York Times*

Lionel Davidson

THE MENORAH MEN P 592, $2.84
"Of his fellow thriller writers, only John Le Carré shows the same instinct for the viscera." —*Chicago Tribune*

NIGHT OF WENCESLAS P 595, $2.84
"A most ingenious thriller, so enriched with style, wit, and a sense of serious comedy that it all but transcends its kind."

—*The New Yorker*

THE ROSE OF TIBET P 593, $2.84
"I hadn't realized how much I missed the genuine Adventure story . . . until I read *The Rose of Tibet*." —Graham Greene

D. M. Devine

MY BROTHER'S KILLER P 558, $2.40
"A most enjoyable crime story which I enjoyed reading down to the last moment."

—Agatha Christie

Kenneth Fearing

THE BIG CLOCK   P 500, $1.95
"It will be some time before chill-hungry clients meet again so rare a
compound of irony, satire, and icy-fingered narrative. *The Big Clock* is
. . . a psychothriller you won't put down."   —*Weekly Book Review*

Andrew Garve

THE ASHES OF LODA   P 430, $1.50
"Garve . . . embellishes a fine fast adventure story with a more credible
picture of the U.S.S.R. than is offered in most thrillers."
                                        —*The New York Times Book Review*

THE CUCKOO LINE AFFAIR   P 451, $1.95
". . . an agreeable and ingenious piece of work."   —*The New Yorker*

A HERO FOR LEANDA   P 429, $1.50
"One can trust Mr. Garve to put a fresh twist to any situation, and the
ending is really a lovely surprise."   —*The Manchester Guardian*

MURDER THROUGH THE LOOKING GLASS   P 449, $1.95
". . . refreshingly out-of-the-way and enjoyable . . . highly recommended
to all comers."   —*Saturday Review*

NO TEARS FOR HILDA   P 441, $1.95
"It starts fine and finishes finer. I got behind on breathing watching Max
get not only his man but his woman, too."   —Rex Stout

THE RIDDLE OF SAMSON   P 450, $1.95
"The story is an excellent one, the people are quite likable, and the
writing is superior."   —*Springfield Republican*

Michael Gilbert

BLOOD AND JUDGMENT   P 446, $1.95
"Gilbert readers need scarcely be told that the characters all come alive
at first sight, and that his surpassing talent for narration enhances any
plot. . . . Don't miss."   —*San Francisco Chronicle*

THE BODY OF A GIRL   P 459, $1.95
"Does what a good mystery should do: open up into all kinds of ramifica-
tions, with untold menace behind the action. At the end, there is a
bang-up climax, and it is a pleasure to see how skilfully Gilbert wraps
everything up."   —*The New York Times Book Review*

THE DANGER WITHIN   P 448, $1.95
"Michael Gilbert has nicely combined some elements of the straight detective story with plenty of action, suspense, and adventure, to produce a superior thriller."   *—Saturday Review*

FEAR TO TREAD   P 458, $1.95
"Merits serious consideration as a work of art."
                                          —The New York Times

Joe Gores

HAMMETT   P 631, $2.84
"Joe Gores at his very best. Terse, powerful writing—with the master, Dashiell Hammett, as the protagonist in a novel I think he would have been proud to call his own."   —Robert Ludlum

C. W. Grafton

BEYOND A REASONABLE DOUBT   P 519, $1.95
"A very ingenious tale of murder . . . a brilliant and gripping narrative."
                    —Jacques Barzun and Wendell Hertig Taylor

THE RAT BEGAN TO GNAW THE ROPE   P 639, $2.84
"Fast, humorous story with flashes of brilliance."
                                          —The New Yorker

Edward Grierson

THE SECOND MAN   P 528, $2.25
"One of the best trial-testimony books to have come along in quite a while."   *—The New Yorker*

Bruce Hamilton

TOO MUCH OF WATER   P 635, $2.84
"A superb sea mystery. . . . The prose is excellent."
  —Jacques Barzun and Wendell Hertig Taylor, *A Catalogue of Crime*

Cyril Hare

DEATH IS NO SPORTSMAN   P 555, $2.40
"You will be thrilled because it succeeds in placing an ingenious story in a new and refreshing setting. . . . The identity of the murderer is really a surprise."   *—Daily Mirror*

Cyril Hare (cont'd)

DEATH WALKS THE WOODS   P 556, $2.40

"Here is a fine formal detective story, with a technically brilliant solution demanding the attention of all connoisseurs of construction."

—Anthony Boucher, *The New York Times Book Review*

AN ENGLISH MURDER   P 455, $2.50

"By a long shot, the best crime story I have read for a long time. Everything is traditional, but originality does not suffer. The setting is perfect. Full marks to Mr. Hare."   —*Irish Press*

SUICIDE EXCEPTED   P 636, $2.84

"Adroit in its manipulation . . . and distinguished by a plot-twister which I'll wager Christie wishes she'd thought of."

—*The New York Times*

TENANT FOR DEATH   P 570, $2.84

"The way in which an air of probability is combined both with clear, terse narrative and with a good deal of subtle suburban atmosphere, proves the extreme skill of the writer."   —*The Spectator*

TRAGEDY AT LAW   P 522, $2.25

"An extremely urbane and well-written detective story."

—*The New York Times*

UNTIMELY DEATH   P 514, $2.25

"The English detective story at its quiet best, meticulously underplayed, rich in perceivings of the droll human animal and ready at the last with a neat surprise which has been there all the while had we but wits to see it."   —*New York Herald Tribune Book Review*

THE WIND BLOWS DEATH   P 589, $2.84

"A plot compounded of musical knowledge, a Dickens allusion, and a subtle point in law is related with delightfully unobtrusive wit, warmth, and style."   —*The New York Times*

WITH A BARE BODKIN   P 523, $2.25

"One of the best detective stories published for a long time."

—*The Spectator*

Robert Harling

THE ENORMOUS SHADOW   P 545, $2.50

"In some ways the best spy story of the modern period. . . . The writing is terse and vivid . . . the ending full of action . . . altogether first-rate."

—Jacques Barzun and Wendell Hertig Taylor, *A Catalogue of Crime*

Matthew Head

THE CABINDA AFFAIR P 541, $2.25
"An absorbing whodunit and a distinguished novel of atmosphere."
—Anthony Boucher, *The New York Times*

THE CONGO VENUS P 597, $2.84
"Terrific. The dialogue is just plain wonderful."
—*The Boston Globe*

MURDER AT THE FLEA CLUB P 542, $2.50
"The true delight is in Head's style, its limpid ease combined with humor
and an awesome precision of phrase." —*San Francisco Chronicle*

M. V. Heberden

ENGAGED TO MURDER P 533, $2.25
"Smooth plotting." —*The New York Times*

James Hilton

WAS IT MURDER? P 501, $1.95
"The story is well planned and well written."
—*The New York Times*

P. M. Hubbard

HIGH TIDE P 571, $2.40
"A smooth elaboration of mounting horror and danger."
—*Library Journal*

Elspeth Huxley

THE AFRICAN POISON MURDERS P 540, $2.25
"Obscure venom, manical mutilations, deadly bush fire, thrilling climax
compose major opus.... Top-flight."
—*Saturday Review of Literature*

MURDER ON SAFARI P 587, $2.84
"Right now we'd call Mrs. Huxley a dangerous rival to Agatha Christie." —*Books*

Francis Iles

BEFORE THE FACT   P 517, $2.50

"Not many 'serious' novelists have produced character studies to compare with Iles's internally terrifying portrait of the murderer in *Before the Fact,* his masterpiece and a work truly deserving the appellation of unique and beyond price."   —Howard Haycraft

MALICE AFORETHOUGHT   P 532, $1.95

"It is a long time since I have read anything so good as *Malice Aforethought,* with its cynical humour, acute criminology, plausible detail and rapid movement. It makes you hug yourself with pleasure."

—H. C. Harwood, *Saturday Review*

Michael Innes

THE CASE OF THE JOURNEYING BOY   P 632, $3.12

"I could see no faults in it. There is no one to compare with him."
—*Illustrated London News*

DEATH BY WATER   P 574, $2.40

"The amount of ironic social criticism and deft characterization of scenes and people would serve another author for six books."

—Jacques Barzun and Wendell Hertig Taylor

HARE SITTING UP   P 590, $2.84

"There is hardly anyone (in mysteries or mainstream) more exquisitely literate, allusive and Jamesian—and hardly anyone with a firmer sense of melodramatic plot or a more vigorous gift of storytelling."

—Anthony Boucher, *The New York Times*

THE LONG FAREWELL   P 575, $2.40

"A model of the deft, classic detective story, told in the most wittily diverting prose."   —*The New York Times*

THE MAN FROM THE SEA   P 591, $2.84

"The pace is brisk, the adventures exciting and excitingly told, and above all he keeps to the very end the interesting ambiguity of the man from the sea."   —*New Statesman*

THE SECRET VANGUARD   P 584, $2.84

"Innes . . . has mastered the art of swift, exciting and well-organized narrative."   —*The New York Times*

THE WEIGHT OF THE EVIDENCE   P 633, $2.84

"First-class puzzle, deftly solved. University background interesting and amusing."   —*Saturday Review of Literature*

Mary Kelly

THE SPOILT KILL   P 565, $2.40

"Mary Kelly is a new Dorothy Sayers. . . . [An] exciting new novel."
—*Evening News*

Lange Lewis

THE BIRTHDAY MURDER   P 518, $1.95

"Almost perfect in its playlike purity and delightful prose."
—Jacques Barzun and Wendell Hertig Taylor

Allan MacKinnon

HOUSE OF DARKNESS   P 582, $2.84

"His best . . . a perfect compendium."
—Jacques Barzun & Wendell Hertig Taylor, *A Catalogue of Crime*

Arthur Maling

LUCKY DEVIL   P 482, $1.95

"The plot unravels at a fast clip, the writing is breezy and Maling's
approach is as fresh as today's stockmarket quotes."
—*Louisville Courier Journal*

RIPOFF   P 483, $1.95

"A swiftly paced story of today's big business is larded with intrigue as
a Ralph Nader-type investigates an insurance scandal and is soon on the
run from a hired gun and his brother. . . . Engrossing and credible."
—*Booklist*

SCHROEDER'S GAME   P 484, $1.95

"As the title indicates, this Schroeder is up to something, and the un-
ravelling of his game is a diverting and sufficiently blood-soaked entertainment."   —*The New Yorker*

Austin Ripley

MINUTE MYSTERIES   P 387, $2.50

More than one hundred of the world's shortest detective stories. Only
one possible solution to each case!

Thomas Sterling

THE EVIL OF THE DAY   P 529, $2.50

"Prose as witty and subtle as it is sharp and clear. . .characters unconven-
tionally conceived and richly bodied forth . . . . In short, a novel to be
treasured."   —Anthony Boucher, *The New York Times*

Julian Symons

THE BELTING INHERITANCE   P 468, $1.95
"A superb whodunit in the best tradition of the detective story."
                              —August Derleth, *Madison Capital Times*

BLAND BEGINNING   P 469, $1.95
"Mr. Symons displays a deft storytelling skill, a quiet and literate wit,
a nice feeling for character, and detectival ingenuity of a high order."
                              —Anthony Boucher, *The New York Times*

BOGUE'S FORTUNE   P 481, $1.95
"There's a touch of the old sardonic humour, and more than a touch of
style."   —*The Spectator*

THE BROKEN PENNY   P 480, $1.95
"The most exciting, astonishing and believable spy story to appear in
years.   —Anthony Boucher, *The New York Times Book Review*

THE COLOR OF MURDER   P 461, $1.95
"A singularly unostentatious and memorably brilliant detective story."
                              —*New York Herald Tribune Book Review*

Dorothy Stockbridge Tillet
(John Stephen Strange)

THE MAN WHO KILLED FORTESCUE   P 536, $2.25
"Better than average."   —*Saturday Review of Literature*

Simon Troy

THE ROAD TO RHUINE   P 583, $2.84
"Unusual and agreeably told."   —*San Francisco Chronicle*

SWIFT TO ITS CLOSE   P 546, $2.40
"A nicely literate British mystery . . . the atmosphere and the plot are
exceptionally well wrought, the dialogue excellent."   —*Best Sellers*

Henry Wade

THE DUKE OF YORK'S STEPS   P 588, $2.84
"A classic of the golden age."
   —Jacques Barzun & Wendell Hertig Taylor, *A Catalogue of Crime*

A DYING FALL   P 543, $2.50
"One of those expert British suspense jobs . . . it crackles with undercur-
rents of blackmail, violent passion and murder. Topnotch in its class."
                                                        —*Time*

If you enjoyed this book you'll want to know about
THE PERENNIAL LIBRARY MYSTERY SERIES

Buy them at your local bookstore or use this coupon for ordering:

Qty	P number	Price
————	————	————
————	————	————
————	————	————
————	————	————
————	————	————
————	————	————
————	————	————
————	————	————
————	————	————
————	————	————
————	————	————
————	————	————
————	————	————

postage and handling charge $1.00
———— book(s) @ $0.25   ————

TOTAL

Prices contained in this coupon are Harper & Row invoice prices only.
They are subject to change without notice, and in no way reflect the prices at
which these books may be sold by other suppliers.

**HARPER & ROW, Mail Order Dept. #PMS, 10 East 53rd St., New
York, N.Y. 10022.**
Please send me the books I have checked above. I am enclosing $————
which includes a postage and handling charge of $1.00 for the first book and
25¢ for each additional book. Send check or money order. No cash or
C.O.D.s please

Name————————————————————————————

Address—————————————————————————————

City———————— State———————— Zip————————
Please allow 4 weeks for delivery. USA only. This offer expires 11/30/84.
Please add applicable sales tax.